The Ragamuffin Mystery

Enid Blyton

The Ragamuffin Mystery

Illustrated by Eric Rowe

AWARD PUBLICATIONS LIMITED

For further information on Enid Blyton
please visit *www.blyton.com*

ISBN 978-1-84135-733-1

First published 1951 by William Collins Sons & Co. Ltd
First published by Award Publications Limited 2003
This edition first published 2009

Published by Award Publications Limited,
The Old Riding School, The Welbeck Estate,
Worksop, Nottinghamshire, S80 3LR

11 2

Printed in the United Kingdom

CONTENTS

1

Off In the Caravan

"This is going to be just about the most exciting holiday we've ever had!" said Roger, carrying a suitcase and bag down to the front door. "Diana, bring that pile of books, will you, before we forget them."

Diana picked them up and ran down the stairs after Roger. At the front door stood a caravan. Diana stood and gloated over it for the twentieth time.

"Fancy Dad buying a caravan!" she said. "And, oh, what a pity he can't come with us, after all!"

"Yes – after all our plans," said Roger. "Still, it's a good thing Mum didn't back out when she heard Dad had to go to America – I was awfully afraid she would! My heart went into my boots, I can tell you."

"Same here," said Diana, stacking the books neatly on a shelf in the caravan. "Have we got our bird-book? We'll see plenty of birds on our travels and that's my holiday task – writing an essay on 'Birds I have seen'."

"Well, don't forget to take the binoculars then," said Roger. "They're hanging in the hall. I say – what did you think about Mum asking Miss Pepper to come with us, now that Dad can't manage?"

Miss Pepper was an old friend of their mother's. The children were fond of her – but Roger felt rather doubtful about having her on a caravan holiday with them. "You see – she's all right in a house," he said to Diana. "But in a small caravan, with hardly any room – won't she get fussed? We shall be so much on top of one another."

"Oh well – Mummy must have someone to take turns at driving the car when it's pulling the caravan," said Diana. "And she'll be company for Mummy, too. She's quite good fun – if only she won't keep making us be tidy, and wash our hands and knees a dozen times a day, and . . ."

"What are you two gossiping about?" said their mother, hurrying out to the caravan with some more things. "If we're going to start off at eleven, we'd better hurry! We've got to pick Miss Pepper up at two o'clock, you know – and if we don't start punctually we'll have to go too fast for a car towing a caravan!"

"I wish Daddy was coming," groaned Diana, helping her mother to pack in more

luggage. "Miss Pepper's all right – but Daddy's such fun on a holiday."

"Yes – it's a pity," said her mother. "But at least we haven't got to put up with Snubby this time!"

"Gosh yes! Snubby with us in a small caravan – and Loony too – would be just about the limit!" said Roger. "Who's he staying with these hols?"

Snubby was their cousin, a ginger-haired, freckled, snub-nosed, twelve-year-old boy. He had no father or mother, and so he spent his holidays with one or other of his aunts and uncles. Snubby by himself was bad enough, but with his quite mad dog, Loony, a beautiful black spaniel, he was enough to drive even the most patient aunt and uncle out of their minds.

"He's staying with Auntie Pat, I think," said Diana. "Isn't he, Mummy? I bet he's driving her crazy. Last time he stayed with her, Loony got a passion for wellies, and he took every single one from the hall cupboard and hid them in the rhododendron bushes . . ."

"And the gardener couldn't believe his eyes when he saw them, and he called Snubby, and Snubby asked him why he had sown welly seed under the rhododendrons!" said Roger, with a sudden snort of laughter.

"Good old Snubby! He is a pest, but honestly, you can't help laughing at him half the time," said Diana. "I bet he wishes he was coming on this caravan holiday with us."

"Well, thank goodness he's not," said their mother. "Pack those rugs in the corner there, Diana. I really think that's about all. Now I'll go in and see that we've got absolutely everything – and if we have we'd better start."

She hurried indoors. Diana looked round the neat little caravan, wondering how long it would be before it was anything but neat! She and her mother and Miss Pepper were to sleep in it at night, and Roger was to sleep in the back of the car. What fun to travel round the countryside, going where they liked – not knowing what county they would sleep in at night – waking up when they liked. Yes – this was going to be something like a holiday!

"There's just one thing I do wish," said Diana to Roger, as they went indoors to say goodbye to their daily help. "I wish and wish that old Barney was coming with us."

"Gosh – so do I!" said Roger. "And Miranda too. Dear little Miranda. We haven't seen her for ages." Miranda was Barney's pet monkey.

"Well, Barney's been travelling about with his father," said Diana. "I wonder if he often thinks how he travelled about before – you know, when he was a child and didn't know who his father was, and went about with the people of circuses and fairs. He did plenty of travelling then!"

"And now he's found his father and a real family of his own, and he's no longer a poor circus boy, all alone in the world," said Roger. "And Miranda isn't a lonely little monkey, going everywhere with him, often hungry and cold – but a spoilt little pet, loved by every single one of Barney's family! And thank goodness, Barney hasn't changed a bit."

"No – he's still the same kind, strong Barney," said Diana. "I do hope we see him these hols. Mummy! Mummy, where are you? We really ought to start, you know."

"Just coming!" called their mother, hurrying downstairs. "I remembered I must find the sunscreen, in case we all get too burnt for words, in this hot weather. Go and say goodbye, dears – and then we'll start."

At last they were in the car, and it moved slowly towards the front gate, pulling the caravan behind it. Fortunately the gates were wide and the posts were not even scraped. Away they went down the lane, the caravan running smoothly behind them, rocking just a little now and again when they went over a rut. Soon they were out on the main road – the holiday had begun!

They stopped for a picnic lunch on the way, and then drove on towards Miss Pepper's. "We shall be late," said Roger, "but it doesn't matter, Mum – Miss Pepper would be most surprised if we arrived punctually!"

"I dare say – but she's sure to be quite ready ten minutes beforehand," said his mother. "And I shall feel just as I used to when she looked after me in my teens – very, very guilty!"

Miss Pepper was waiting for them on her doorstep, her suitcases beside her. She looked as tall and thin as ever, but her eyes twinkled as usual behind their glasses, and she smiled warmly.

"Well, here you all are, bless you!" she said. "And wonder of wonders not more than fifteen minutes late! Had your lunch?"

"Yes, Miss Pepper," said everyone, and Roger leaped out to take her luggage. He stowed it away in the caravan.

"What a fine caravan!" said Miss Pepper approvingly. "Well, well – I never thought I'd ever sleep in a caravan and here I am, quite looking forward to it!"

"I'll drive on for some way," said the children's mother. "Then you can take a short turn at driving if you will. We thought we'd make for that lovely little lake at Yesterley. The children can swim then. Isn't it a mercy it's such glorious weather?"

"It certainly is," said Miss Pepper, settling herself in the front seat. "Dear me – it seems strange not to have Snubby with us.

He's always come with the children when I've been with them before."

"He's staying with Auntie Pat – and I expect he's driving her mad," said Diana. "All the same, I wish his dog Loony was with us – darling Loony, I do love him."

"Hm," said Miss Pepper, doubtfully. "I'm fond of him too – but I don't think I should be fond of him long if he went for a caravan holiday with us. He's not a very restful dog."

It was very pleasant driving along on that sunny day, with three weeks stretching before them, lazy, lovely weeks, full of picnics, swimming, ice creams – and perhaps sleeping out in the open air instead of in the caravan. Roger made up his mind to suggest it that very first night – not for his mother or Miss Pepper, just for himself and Diana.

The car purred on and on – where would they stop for the night? Nobody knew and nobody cared. The caravan rolled on behind them, and every now and again Roger looked back to make sure it was still safely there.

"We're going to have fun!" he said to Diana. "For three whole weeks – nothing but fun!"

2

Very Unexpected!

For five days Roger and Diana had a truly wonderful time. For two nights they stayed by the lovely blue lake at Yesterley, and picnicked and swam. Miss Pepper surprised them all by producing a swimsuit and swimming too – and what was more she was a very good swimmer indeed!

"Goodness!" said Diana, lying panting on the white sand that edged the lake. "Goodness! I had a swimming race with Miss Pepper – and she beat me. And look, she's still swimming, and I've had to come out and rest."

"She's very good," said Roger. "So's Mum, actually. I wish I could float as long as she can – she just goes on and on and yet it's not salt water! She must waggle her hands about or something."

"This is just the kind of holiday I like," said Diana. "Wasn't it fun last night, sleeping out on the heather? Did you hear that owl hooting just by us? It was so loud. It nearly made me jump out of my skin."

"Didn't hear a thing," said Roger. "I just shut my eyes and never knew anything until you shook me awake this morning. How long are Mum and Miss Pepper staying in the water? I'm hungry."

They were all hungry those first five days, even Miss Pepper, who became quite ashamed of the enormous appetite she suddenly discovered.

"I do wish you wouldn't look so surprised, you two, when I take a third helping," she said. "You make me feel greedy – and really, it's only just that I'm very hungry."

"Aha! Snubby would like to hear you say that!" said Roger. "You always used to tell him he wasn't really hungry when he wanted a third helping – but just plain greedy!"

"Dear Snubby!" said Miss Pepper. "I do wonder how he is getting on these holidays. Let me see now – your Auntie Pat hasn't any children, has she, so Snubby won't have anyone to play with. I'm afraid he may make himself a bit of a nuisance."

"More than a bit," said Diana. "He can behave like a lunatic when he's bored. He thinks of the most awful things to do. Don't you remember how he thought he'd sweep our chimney one day, when it smoked a little, and then—"

"Don't talk of it," said her mother, with a groan. "I can't bear even to remember that day. I know your father nearly went mad, and chased Snubby round and round the garden with the chimney brush."

"And fell over Loony," said Diana.

"Yes. Funny the way Loony always gets under the feet of anyone who's angry with Snubby," said Roger. "Remarkably clever dog, Loony."

Each night the four of them sat in the caravan and listened to the news on the radio. They hadn't seen a single newspaper since they had set off on their holiday, but as Miss Pepper said, it didn't do to cut themselves off completely from everything.

"Someone might have landed on Mars – or started a war – or had an earthquake," said Miss Pepper. "We had better listen just once a day."

On the fifth night, they were as usual sitting in the caravan, listening to the evening news on the little radio. The children listened with only half an ear, until the announcer came to the weather. That was really important! Was the weather still going to be warm and sunny?

The news came to an end. It had been very dull – a new strike – a long speech by somebody important – a new kind of aeroplane tested – and then there came a message that made them all sit up at once.

Miss Pepper was just about to turn off the radio, when the voice spoke urgently.

"Here is a message for Mrs Susan Lynton, who is on a caravan tour with her children. Will she please telephone 01392 68251 at once, as her sister is dangerously ill. I will repeat that. Here is a message for . . ."

No one spoke for a few seconds, or even moved, as the message was repeated. Then Diana whispered. "Mummy – it's us they are trying to reach! You're Susan Lynton – and oh Mummy, does it mean . . .?"

"It means that something's happened to your mother's sister – your Aunt Pat," said Miss Pepper, getting up at once. "Don't worry too much, my dear – we'll drive straight off to a telephone box and find out what's wrong."

"Oh dear – what can have happened?" said Mrs Lynton, looking very pale. "I'll have to go back – I'll have to go to Pat. Oh, I feel quite stunned."

The children felt stunned too. What a dreadful thing to happen in the middle of a lovely holiday! Poor Auntie Pat – what could have happened? "Dangerously ill" – that sounded very frightening.

"You two children stay here in the caravan," said Miss Pepper, briskly, taking charge as usual. "I'll drive your mother to the nearest village and we'll telephone. We'll get back here as soon as possible. Cheer up,

Diana – don't look so upset, dear. It may not be as bad as it sounds."

In ten minutes, Miss Pepper was driving the car down the lane, the children's mother sitting silently beside her. Roger and Diana watched them go, then went and sat down outside the caravan in the heather. Diana was crying.

Roger gave her a quick hug. "It might not be so bad," he said. "I expect Mum will have to go back, though. We'll have to as well, I suppose."

"But how can we?" wept Diana. "We'd be on our own."

"I'd forgotten that. And what about old Snubby?" said Roger. "He can't stay at

Auntie Pat's if she's ill – or gone to hospital. What's to happen to him?"

"And to us too," said Diana. "Mummy will certainly stay to look after Auntie Pat. She's so fond of her. Oh, what an awful thing to happen in the middle of such a lovely holiday!"

It seemed a very long time before their mother came back with Miss Pepper. The sun had gone down. The children heard the car coming in the darkness and stood up at once. They ran to it as soon as their mother got out.

But it wasn't their mother! It was Miss Pepper – and it wasn't their car either, it was a taxi!

"Oh! What's happened? Where's Mummy?" cried Diana.

"Gone off in the car to see to your auntie," said Miss Pepper, paying the taxi driver. "She's had a fall and hurt her head, and the doctors thought she might die. But they've just given your mother a better report of her, and have asked her to get back as soon as she can, as your aunt keeps calling for her."

"Oh! Poor Mummy!" said Diana, thinking of her mother driving fast through the night, all alone, worrying about her sister. "Oh, Miss Pepper – do you think Auntie Pat will be all right?"

"From the doctor's latest report, I should

think she will," said Miss Pepper, comfortingly. "So don't fret too much. It's silly to cross bridges before you come to them. Mummy sent you her love, and she says she'll give us the latest news in the morning, if I go into the village to telephone. It's not very far."

"Will Mum come back here, and go on with our holiday?" asked Roger.

"No. No, I think I can say that quite definitely," said Miss Pepper. "I'm pretty sure she will want to stay with your Aunt Pat till she's really on the mend. We had no time to decide exactly what to do – but I'm afraid you'll have to put up with me for a bit, my dears! I promised your mother I'd be with you till she can have you home again."

"But what are our plans now, then?" asked Roger feeling rather dazed. "We've this caravan – but no car – and our house is shut up. Will we leave the caravan here and go and stay with you, Miss Pepper?"

"I really do not know, Roger dear," said Miss Pepper. "Shall we leave everything till tomorrow? Things like this do happen, you know, and then we often find out how strong – or weak – we are! Your mother, now, was full of courage as soon as she got over the shock; she was ready to face up to anything!"

"What about poor Snubby?" said Diana. "He's staying with Auntie Pat. Oh, Miss

Pepper – Auntie Pat didn't fall over Loony, did she?"

"No – she slipped off a ladder," said Miss Pepper. "Now, I'm going to open a bottle of fizzy orange, and find those chocolate biscuits and macaroons we had left over from lunch and we're going to have a nice little supper."

The two children felt glad to have Miss Pepper with them. She was cheerful and brisk, and even made one or two little jokes. Roger felt more cheerful too, after his supper, but Diana was still scared and upset.

"Roger, would you like to sleep in your mother's bunk tonight in the caravan with Diana and me?" Miss Pepper asked. "I expect Diana would like you in here with us tonight."

"Yes. Yes. I'd like to sleep here instead of in the open," said Roger, and Diana nodded, pleased. Now if she was awake in the night and felt scared and sad, she could talk to Roger. Brothers were good to have when things went wrong!

Soon the caravan was in darkness, while three people tried to get to sleep. What news would the morning bring? Good – or bad? And what was going to happen to their holiday?

3

Good Old Barney

Next morning Miss Pepper was up bright and early, and woke the two children. "Wake up!" she said. "We'll have breakfast and then I'll pop down to the village and telephone your mother. Did you sleep well?"

"Yes, I did," said Diana, rather surprised, for she had felt sure that she wouldn't sleep at all. Roger had slept well too, and both of them felt more ready to face up to whatever news they would hear.

Miss Pepper made the tea, and Diana cut the bread. Soon they were eating cold ham, and drinking the hot tea. "Though really, why we don't have fizzy orange this hot morning, instead of this scalding tea, I can't think!" said Diana.

Immediately after breakfast Miss Pepper set off briskly to the village. She was back in half an hour and the children, who were anxiously looking out for her, ran to meet her, most relieved to see a smile on her face.

"Better news," said Miss Pepper at once.

"Your mother arrived safely, and your aunt was so glad to see her – and she has taken a turn for the better already."

"Good, good!" said Diana, thankfully.

"Apparently she fell from the top of a ladder when she was tying up some ramblers on the wall," said Miss Pepper. "And she hit her head on the stone path. Nothing to do with Loony at all! She's in hospital, and your mother is with her. And I'm afraid your mother will have to stay away for quite a while, because there is no one to look after your uncle – so your mother says she'll spend part of her time seeing to your uncle and the other part with your aunt."

"Oh. Then what's to happen to us?" said Diana at once.

"Well, I suppose I'll have to try and hire a car and take the caravan back to my own home," said Miss Pepper. "You'll have to come with me, I'm afraid, as your own house is shut up. I'm sorry, dears – very very sorry. This is a horrible end to what was going to be one of your very best holidays. But I honestly don't see what else we can do."

"I don't either," said Roger gloomily. "And I think it's jolly good of you to take all this trouble for us, Miss Pepper. I'm sure you don't want us in your little house! Oh dear – isn't this all horrid!"

"Diana can come with me to find out

about a car," said Miss Pepper as they cleared up the caravan and made up the bunks. "And Roger can stay here with the caravan. That be all right, Roger?"

"Of course," said Roger, still gloomy, and watched Miss Pepper go off to the village again, Diana by her side. What a mess up of a glorious holiday! Miss Pepper was good and kind – but the thought of living for two or three weeks in her tidy little house filled Roger with dread.

"We'll be too bored for words!" he thought and then reproached himself for being unkind. Whatever would they have done without Miss Pepper just now! "We might have gone to stay with old Barney, if he hadn't been touring the country with his father," his thoughts ran on. "Oh well – we'll just have to make the best of things, I suppose."

Miss Pepper and Diana came back in an hour's time, looking depressed.

"We can't get a car anywhere in the village," said Miss Pepper. "So we phoned the nearest town, and somebody is going to try there for us. I do hope we shan't have to take some old crock that will break down halfway home! I'm not really very good at driving cars I don't know."

Their caravan was set on a heathery hill, just off the road, not far from a farmhouse. The farmer had given them permission to stay on the hill – and about three o'clock that afternoon, the three saw him coming up to their caravan.

"Oh dear – I hope he's not going to turn us off!" said Miss Pepper in a fright.

The farmer came slowly up to where they were all sitting outside the caravan, his dog at his heels.

"Good afternoon, ma'am," he said, in his pleasant country voice. "There's a message for you, sent to my farmhouse by the post office."

He held out the envelope and Miss Pepper took it, suddenly frightened. She tore it open and read it. Then she looked round at the two waiting children, puzzled.

"Listen," she said, "it says – 'Wait till you see us tonight, Barney'."

"Wait till you see us tonight!" echoed Diana, and her face suddenly lit up. "Oh, Miss Pepper! Barney and his father must have heard about Auntie Pat's accident, and how Mummy had to go to her, leaving us here! And they're coming here tonight! Oh, how wonderful!"

"They must have heard the message on the radio last night, when we did!" said Roger. "And they rang the telephone number and found out what was happening. Miss Pepper! Everything will be all right now! Barney's father will arrange about a car and everything. Oh, thank goodness!"

Diana gave a long sigh of relief, and her heart suddenly lightened. Barney was coming – and his nice father. Now things would soon be settled for them. Perhaps they could go and stay with Barney.

"Thank you," said Miss Pepper to the farmer, and he nodded, and left, with his dog still at his heels.

"Wait till you see us tonight!" said Diana, quoting the message again. "That must mean that they are driving straight to us, wherever they are – and must be rather far away, or they would arrive before tonight. Good old Barney! Now we can just sit back and not worry."

"You two had better go down to the river and have a swim," said Miss Pepper. "It's so hot today. I won't come with you, because someone had better stay with the caravan. Go along now, and have a good swim. It will do you good."

So off went Roger and Diana, feeling considerably happier because of Barney's message. How good it was to have friends – how very good!

"We shall see dear little Miranda too," said Diana happily. "The best thing about animals is that they don't seem to change, as human beings do! Miranda must have looked the same ever since she was a year old!"

They had a long swim, and then lay in

the warm heather to dry. They were hungry when they got back to the caravan. "Any news of Barney yet? Or another message?" asked Roger. Miss Pepper shook her head.

"No – but Barney said 'tonight' in his message, you know. We shall have to wait in patience. I'm sure they must be down in Cornwall, or up in the north of Scotland or in the Welsh mountains – somewhere quite far away from here, anyway."

"I'm not going to bed till they come," said Roger firmly.

"I can't really expect you to!" said Miss Pepper. "But I hope it's before twelve o'clock!"

The evening drew on, and the sun began to sink low down in the west. At every far off sound of a car going by on a distant road, the three of them stiffened and listened – but car after car purred by in the distance and not one stopped, or came in their direction.

Then at last, just as it was getting really dark, the sound of a car jolting over the rough road next to the old farmhouse came to their ears. "That must be Barney!" said Diana in excitement. They listened anxiously.

The car stopped – and then, a few minutes later they heard it starting up again in the silence of the evening. It was coming over the rough track that led to them!

"It's Barney! It must be!" cried Roger,

leaping up. "The villagers must have sent them to the farm, and the farmer has told them where we are. Barney! Barney! Barney!"

An answering shout came to their ears. "Hey! We're coming! The track's rough, though!"

Soon a big car came to a stop beside the caravan, and a tall figure leaped out; Roger and Diana ran to meet it – and to greet dear old Barney, with little Miranda the monkey on his shoulder, chattering excitedly.

"Hello, hello!" cried Barney, and hugged

both Diana and Roger. "Sorry to be so long coming – we were right away in Scotland! Heard the news on the radio last night, of course, and phoned your mother. How are you?"

"Oh, Barney, it's so lovely to see you," said Diana. "We simply didn't know what to do when Mummy had to go off and leave us. Is that your father getting out of the car now?"

"Yes. We can leave everything to him," said Barney, very happy to be with his friends again. "Every single thing! He's got a marvellous plan. Hello, Miss Pepper. Isn't this a surprise?"

"It certainly is," said Miss Pepper. "Ah, here's your father! Good evening – it is good of you to come to us like this!"

"We'll soon fix up some plans," said Barney's father, shaking hands. "Sorry about this trouble. Let's go into that caravan of yours and talk."

And in they all went, Miranda the monkey too, chattering loudly, leaping from one shoulder to another and making Roger and Diana laugh in glee. Good old Barney – dear little Miranda – it really was wonderful to see them again!

4

A Wonderful Idea

It seemed quite a crowd in the little caravan. Miss Pepper lit the lamp, and they all looked at one another, blinking. Barney's brilliant blue eyes shone as he looked round at everyone. He was as brown as a berry, as usual, and his grin just as wide as ever!

His father spoke to Miss Pepper. "We rang up again tonight to see how Mrs Lynton's sister was, and she is just a little better and will certainly recover well now – but it will take time."

"Thank goodness it's better news," said Miss Pepper. "It was such a terrible shock last night. I am so glad to see you, Mr Martin – I really was worried about what to do for the best."

"Well, don't worry any more," said Mr Martin. "What I propose is that I should hitch your caravan on to my car and—"

"And take us home?" said Roger. "But our house is shut up, Mr Martin!"

"Yes, I know that," said Barney's father.

"And I know too that it must be a great disappointment to you, to have your three weeks holiday broken up – so I think that if you all joined Barney – or let him join you, whichever way you like to put it – that would solve your difficulties."

"You mean we could have your car to drive the caravan about?" asked Miss Pepper. "Oh dear – if you mean me to drive it, Mr Martin, I'm afraid I couldn't. It's so big and—"

"No, no – I didn't mean that," said Mr Martin. "I'll explain. Barney and I are on a week's holiday and it's almost up, because I have to get back. What I propose is that I hitch up your caravan, and we go off tomorrow and find some really nice place for you all to stay in – somewhere near a little inn, perhaps, so that you and Diana can sleep indoors there, and the two boys can sleep in the caravan, and—"

"Oh! What a wonderful idea!" said Diana, her eyes shining. "Some place by the sea, perhaps?"

"We'll see," said Mr Martin, smiling at her excited face. "If we can find a good spot tomorrow, I'll leave you all there, with the caravan, and drive back home. Miss Pepper will keep an eye on you, I know! When the time comes for you to leave, I'll drive up and fetch the caravan. What do you think of that?"

"Oh – too good to be true!" said Roger. "I honestly thought we'd have to go home and look after ourselves in an empty house! It's awfully good of you, Mr Martin, and of course, solves all our problems – except one!"

"And what problem's that?" asked Mr Martin.

"Well – about Snubby," said Roger. "What's going to happen to him?"

"Can't he come with us?" said Diana, eagerly. "There's room in the caravan for three – or he could sleep in whatever inn or hotel Miss Pepper and I go to."

"Dear me – I'd forgotten about Snubby!" said Mr Martin. "Of course he can come too. He was staying with the aunt who's ill, wasn't he, poor fellow. We'll telephone your mother and tell her to send him up to us, when we've decided where you're going to stay."

Diana heaved a great sigh. "I was so worried about everything," she said. "And now all the troubles are smoothed out. Thank you very much, Mr Martin. And to think we'll have Barney and Miranda with us too! Miranda, do you hear that? You're coming on holiday with us now!"

Miranda heard her name, and chattered in delight. She leaped to Diana's shoulder and pulled her hair gently, pretending to whisper something into her ear.

"You dear, funny little thing," said Diana, fondling her. "Fancy having you with us too – what a treat!"

"Can I offer you some cocoa – or some orangeade?" asked Miss Pepper. "I'm afraid there's nothing very exciting to give you for supper."

"Oh, I nearly forgot!" said Barney, getting up. "We've got a whole lot of stuff in the car. We didn't stop to have meals at hotels today, we just brought bread and ham and fruit and tomatoes, and ate them as we drove along. We so badly wanted to get here as soon as possible. I'll go and bring some of it in."

"How lovely!" said Diana. "I don't know why, but I suddenly feel very hungry."

"It's because your worries are gone, dear!" said Miss Pepper. "I feel a bit hungry myself too! It is truly good of you, Mr Martin, to come to our aid like this."

"Ah well – you've been kind to Barney many a time," said Mr Martin. "Hey, what's that monkey doing?"

"Oh – she's got my sponge!" said Diana with a delighted giggle. "Miranda, give it to me! Oh look, she's washing her face with it, just as she's seen me do at times. Miranda, that's *my* sponge!"

"Now she's put it into her mouth!" said Miss Pepper. "Oh, the naughty little thing! Surely she's not thinking of eating it."

Barney deftly removed the sponge and scolded the little monkey, who at once covered her face with her arms, and sat in a corner giving little moans.

"Don't pretend like that!" said Barney, going out of the caravan. "You're not a bit sorry. I'll be back in half a jiffy, everyone. See Miranda doesn't get your soap, Di!"

Barney was soon back with paper bags and tins. Then they all settled down to a first-rate supper of ham, tomatoes, cheese, ripe plums and orangeade.

"What are you going to do tonight – about sleeping, I mean?" said Miss Pepper to Mr Martin. "It's such a lovely night, I expect the children will sleep out of doors again, on the heather, with a rug round them. But you won't want to do that, Mr Martin."

"No, I'd rather go to the little inn in the village," said Barney's father. "Barney can stay here with you, of course. I'd like to telephone Mrs Lynton tonight and tell her we'll have Snubby as soon as we can. Tomorrow we'll decide where we'll go and then I'll let Mrs Lynton know where to send Snubby. Well – I'll say goodnight, I think. I can see Diana yawning her head off!"

"Goodnight," said Roger, "and thanks very much. See you tomorrow!" Everyone went to the car to see Mr Martin off, and soon he was jolting slowly over the little track that led back to the farmhouse.

"And now it's bed for all of us," said Miss Pepper briskly. "My word, I feel different now – everything's straightened out so well! I just wish your mother hadn't had her holiday spoilt, though she won't mind so long as your aunt is on the mend!"

The two boys went out to find a thick patch of heather. "We'll wash in the stream tomorrow morning," yawned Roger, settling down on a rug. "Here – there's enough rug for you and Miranda, Barney."

Miranda cuddled up into Barney's neck, chattering in his ear. He was sleepy and didn't answer, and she tweaked his hair.

"Now look here, Miranda," said Barney, undoing her tiny fingers from his hair. "I will not have you pulling my hair when I want to go to sleep. Settle down!"

And Miranda settled down meekly, her small brown face hidden in his neck. Barney patted her and smiled. What a funny little thing she was!

Miss Pepper and Diana slept in the caravan with the door wide open for air. Miss Pepper sighed with relief as she closed her eyes. Things were turning out better than she had hoped!

In the morning, quite early, Mr Martin was back again in the car, complete with new-laid eggs, new-made bread, butter and fresh milk from the farm. "And very nice

too!" said Miss Pepper approvingly.
"Miranda – leave that egg alone!"

"I've been looking at a map," said Mr
Martin after breakfast, and spread a large
one out on the heathery ground, where they
had all sat having breakfast in the warm
sun. "The thing we have to decide is where
to go! Any ideas, anyone?"

"Somewhere by the sea," said Roger at
once. "If this hot weather goes on, we'll
want to swim."

"Not in a big town," said Miss Pepper.
"Somewhere small and countrified."

"Somewhere I can watch birds," said Diana. "I've got a holiday essay to write on 'Birds I have seen'."

"Oh, don't start talking about that essay again!" said Roger. "I bet you don't watch for a single bird the whole time!"

Diana glared at him, and Miss Pepper hurriedly interrupted. "There are birds everywhere, Diana – we really don't need to look for any special bird-haunt. Barney, what kind of place would you like?"

"Well – I hate modern holiday spots where there are crowds of people," said Barney. "I'd rather go to some quiet old place – where we can laze about in old clothes, do exactly what we like, and not have to bother with anyone else at all."

"I think we are all pretty well agreed then," said Miss Pepper. "But where shall we find a place like that in the middle of summer? Most places by the sea are so crowded now."

"We'll go somewhere on this hilly Welsh coast, I think," said Mr Martin, tracing a route with his finger. "It's lovely country round there. I vote we start off straightaway and cruise along by the sea, and we'll stop as soon as we find the place we want. Come along – let's pack up and go at once!"

5

A Halt For Ice Creams

Before long they were all on their way. Mr Martin's car was a big one, and there was plenty of room for them all. The caravan swayed along behind, and Mr Martin had to keep remembering that his car was pulling it, and try not to swing round corners too fast!

They drove till lunch-time, and then had a picnic by the roadside, in a little wood. They looked at the map again. "Soon be by the sea," said Mr Martin, following the map with his fingers. "Then we'll look out for a likely spot for you. We'll drive straight through all the big seaside towns, and dawdle along the coast looking for what we want."

"This is fun!" said Diana. "Oh, Miranda – you'll be sick! Barney, that's the fourth plum she's taken."

Barney took away the plum, and Miranda flew into a rage. She leaped on to his head, pulling one of his ears till he shouted. Then she was sorry and tried to creep down his neck, under his shirt.

"Really, you can't help laughing at the naughty little thing!" said Miss Pepper. "What we shall do when Snubby arrives with that mad spaniel Loony, I don't know! There'll be no peace for anybody!"

"Well, I must say I'm pleased we haven't that pair in the car with us yet," said Mr Martin, folding up the map. "A mad dog, an idiotic boy and a naughty monkey would certainly be too much for any driver!"

They drove off again. They came to a big seaside town packed with trippers, noisy and full of litter. "Straight through here," said Mr Martin firmly. "And the next one too. After that we come to a lonely part of the coast, and we'll keep our eyes open."

Through that town they went, and then right through the next, without stopping. Now they were leaving behind the crowded part of the coast, and coming to deserted bays, lonely sweeps of sand, tiny villages, fishing hamlets. Hills rose up from the coast, and the car had to take a roundabout route, going slowly because of the caravan behind it.

"This looks more like what we want," said Diana, looking out of the car window at the sea on one side and hills on the other. "Mr Martin – do you think we could stop for an ice cream sometime? I'm simply too

hot for words, even w…
open!"

"Good idea!" said Mr …
stopped at the next village …
that ran down to the sea. But …
shop that sold ice cream! "You…
Penrhyndendraith," said the wo…
asked. "That's got a good ice crea… …op
there. And if the young ones want a swim,
you tell them to go to Merlin's Cove –
they'll find the best swimming there in the
kingdom."

"That sounds great," said Roger, and they
once more drove on. Round the coast they
went, with the splashing sea on one side,
and the mountains on the other – for now
the hills had grown higher, and some of
them towered up into the sky.

"Grand country!" said Mr Martin. "Now,
where is this Penny-denny-draith place? Ah –
that looks like it – see, built on the slope of
the hill."

They came to Penrhyndendraith. It was a
truly picturesque place, a fishing village,
with a dozen or so old cottages built along
the seafront and others straggling up the
slope of the hill behind.

Above the cottages on the hill rose a
strange old place with curious turrets and
towers. It was set right against a cliff-like
hill, so that the back of it had no windows
at all. Some of it was falling to pieces, and

in places as if only the ivy held it together!

A signboard was set over the great old doorway, but it was too far away for the children to read what was on it. Diana was more interested in finding the ice cream shop than in looking at the half-ruined building on the hill. She jogged Mr Martin's arm gently. "Look – would that be where the ice cream shop is?" she asked, and pointed to the crooked row of cottages.

Mr Martin stopped the car near them. "Well, as I can see only one that looks like a shop, that must be it!" he said. "Yes – see what it says over the door: 'Myfanwy Jones, General Dealer'."

"And look – it says 'Ice cream'!" said Roger. "In the corner of the window, see? Come on – let's get out of the car."

So out they jumped and went to the little shop. What a curious place it was! Inside it was very dark, and there was little space to stand, because of the hundreds of things that the shop sold! The goods were piled on the floor, they hung from the walls, they swung from the ceiling!

"It must sell simply everything in the world!" said Diana in astonishment. "Eatables, drinkables, china, pots and pans, fishing-nets. Miss Pepper, it's like a shop out of an old fairytale!"

"And here's the witch!" whispered Roger,

and got a frown from Miss Pepper, as an old woman shuffled behind the small counter. Her face was a mass of wrinkles, and her snowy white hair was tucked away under a little cap of black net. But old though she looked, her eyes were startlingly bright and piercing.

She spoke to them in Welsh, which they didn't understand. Diana pointed to a card that said "ice cream" and the old lady nodded and smiled suddenly.

"Two scoops? Three? Four?" she said in English.

"Oooh – twenty!" said Roger at once, and everyone laughed, the old woman too.

"How big are your ice creams?" asked Diana. The old woman took a scoop and scooped some from an ice-box – a good large helping, which she slapped into a cone.

"Ah – I think two scoops each will be enough for the children," said Miss Pepper, "and one each for the grown-ups. What about Miranda, Barney?"

"Oh, one for her," said Barney. "She'll probably put most of it on the top of her head, because she's so hot!"

"There is a big seat outside," said the old lady, nodding her head as the children took the ice creams, and they took the hint and went to sit on the hard old wooden bench. Mr Martin and Miranda joined them.

"Not much taste – but very creamy and

deliciously cold," said Barney. "Miranda, please go and sit on the ground. I do not like you to dribble ice cream all down my neck. Nor do I like it held against my ear. Sit on the ground!"

The little monkey leaped down to the ground, chattering, holding her ice cream tightly in her paw. The old lady, who had followed them outside was very interested in Miranda, and stayed there to watch her.

"Very good little monkey," she said, in her lilting Welsh voice. "You come far?"

"Quite a long way," said Barney.

"You go far?" said the old lady.

"We don't know. We are looking for somewhere quiet to stay," said Barney. "Somewhere near here, perhaps. It is such a lovely country. We don't want a big place, with big hotels – but perhaps a quiet old inn, and . . ."

"Ah, then you go up there, see?" said the old lady, and pointed up to the strange, half-ruined place they had seen on the hills. "Quiet, very quiet – and the food is, it is so good, so good. And here it is beautiful, with the sea so blue, and the sand so white, and . . ."

"But – is that old place occupied then?" said Mr Martin, astonished. "I thought it was just an empty ruin."

"No, no – my son – he keeps it," said the old lady proudly. "It is an inn, sir, you understand? And what food! Big men come here, important men —they say how good the food, how good!"

Nobody could believe that important people would stay at the half-ruined place. The old woman saw that they did not believe her, and she grasped Mr Martin's arm.

"I speak the truth," she said. "To my son's inn come Sir Richard Ballinor, and Professor Hallinan, and . . ."

Mr Martin knew those names. "One is a famous botanist and the other is a well-known ornithologist – a man who studies birds," he told the astonished children. He turned to the old lady. "There are many flowers here, then?" he said. "And rare birds?"

"Yes, many, many – up in the hills and round the coves and on the cliffs," said the old lady, nodding her head. "Big men come to study them, I tell you, sir. My son, he knows them all. His cooking pleases them, it is good, very good. You go to stay there too, sir? He has not many people now, it is a good time. Very good cooking."

"Well – we might as well go up and see the old place," said Mr Martin, taking out some money to pay for the ice creams. "Thanks very much, Mrs Jones. We enjoyed your ice creams. Is there a road up to the old inn?"

"It is very rough, sir. You must go slowly," said the old woman, smiling delightedly at the thought that they were really going to see her son's place. "Cooking very good sir, very, very good."

They all went off to their car. "She's got good cooking on the brain," said Roger. "I wonder what the old place is like? It might be fun to stay there – there's all we want here, really – great swimming . . ."

"Wonderful walks, I should think," said Barney, who loved walking. "And a great view."

"Fishing," said Roger, watching a small fishing-boat on the bay, its sails filling out with the wind.

"No trippers," said Miss Pepper.

"And birds for me!" said Diana happily.

"You and your birds!" said Roger scornfully, and Diana immediately gave him a punch.

"Well, up to the inn we go!" said Mr Martin as they started off slowly up the steep track, leaving the caravan behind for the time being. "And what shall we find there, I wonder?"

6

Penrhyndendraith Inn

The car crawled up the steep hill, on the zigzagging track. The higher they went, the more magnificent the views became.

Diana gasped when she looked down the hill and saw the wonderful bay, and the great stretch of heaving sea beyond.

"Oh, look!" she said. "How lucky people are who live in that old inn, Miss Pepper, and look out on that view every day. And see – the view across the hills is glorious too – are those mountains beyond?"

"Yes. And beautiful ones too!" said Miss Pepper. "Did you ever see such a blaze of heather – why, the hills look on fire with it! My goodness me, I can't help hoping that it will be possible for us to stay in the inn. I've never seen such views in my life!"

At last they reached the old inn. It really looked rather like a half-ruined castle! The great sign above the open door gave its name: PENRHYNDENDRAITH INN.

"Goodness knows how it's pronounced,"

said Diana. "I say, isn't it dark inside! What do we do? Ring the bell?"

"Yes, if there is one – but there isn't," said Roger, looking all round. "No knocker either. What do we do? Yell?"

"Is anyone there?" shouted Barney obligingly, and they all jumped at his enormous yell. A small boy with an untidy shock of hair came running round a corner, followed by a great grey goose. He shouted out something in Welsh, and then disappeared into the open doorway, followed by the waddling goose.

"Well – I imagine that he and the goose have gone to find the owner of the inn," said Miss Pepper. "Ah – here comes someone now!"

A lively little woman came hurrying up the hallway to the door, followed by the small boy, the goose still tagging along behind.

"Good afternoon," said Mr Martin politely. "Er – Mrs Jones down in the village told us of this inn, and . . ."

The plump little woman smiled all over her face, and rattled out an answer at top speed.

"Oh yes, sir, yes, sir, that would be my mother-in-law, she knows this place well, and a good inn it is, no doubt about that, sir, we get important people here, you should just peep into our visitors' books, oh, the fine names that are there, and my husband Llewellyn, he is the best cook in the world, he went to London to learn his cooking in one of the big hotels, very good cooking, oh very . . ."

"Er – what I wanted to ask," put in Mr Martin, afraid that the lively woman would never stop, "what I wanted to know was—"

"Oh yes, sir, you ask me anything," said the woman, smiling and nodding. "Come in, won't you, and see what a wonderful place this is, and oh, the cooking, sir, well can you smell what's baking now. That's my husband, he's always cooking, he's . . ."

This sounded exactly as if her husband was being baked, and Diana gave a sudden giggle.

They followed the woman into the great dark entrance hall, the boy and the goose behind them. Talking all the time, she showed them an enormous, rather dilapidated dining-room, and then took them up some stone stairs, uncarpeted, to the bedrooms.

"The beds are comfortable, the view is fine, just you look, sir, did you ever see anything like it?"

Certainly the view was wonderful, and everyone gasped at it. "And we don't charge a great deal, sir," rattled on the little woman. "You come to us if you want to stay in these parts, I tell you the cooking is fine, sir, very good cooking!"

Miranda the monkey stopped the flow of talk quite suddenly, by flinging herself on the grey goose's back. The goose was simply amazed, and began to cackle so loudly that it made everyone jump. The small boy ran to take the monkey off its back, and Miranda promptly jumped on to his shoulder. He screamed in fright and Miranda leaped back to Barney.

"Sorry about that," said Barney to the surprised woman. "It was just that Miranda wanted to see what sort of creature the goose was. I don't believe she's seen one before. Er – is the goose safe?"

The great bird was advancing on him, its enormous wings flapping, cackling at the top of its voice.

"Take Waddle away," said the woman crossly to the small boy. "He must not come indoors. Always I am telling you that." She turned to the others, but before she could begin one of her long speeches again, Mr Martin spoke firmly to her.

"This is my son, and these other children are his friends. This lady, Miss Pepper, is with them, but I go back home today. Another boy, and a dog, will come soon. Can you let them have meals here – and a bed for Miss Pepper and Diana? The others would sleep in a caravan we have."

"Oh, it would be an honour, it would be a pleasure to have them!" cried the talkative little woman. "My names is Jones, sir, Mrs Llewellyn Jones, and certainly we will look after them all, they shall have the best food, they shall go fishing with our men, they shall have picnics – and very good cooking, sir, and . . ."

"Well, thank you," said Mr Martin, and turned to Miss Pepper. "Would you like to stay here, Miss Pepper? I can see already that the children approve!"

"Yes, Mr Martin. I think this is just what we're looking for," said Miss Pepper. "The views and the walks will be enough for me – and as for the children, if they can fish and swim and explore, that's all they'll want! Yes – I'd like to stay here."

"Good, good, good!" cried Diana, and gave Miss Pepper such a sudden hug that she gasped. "And Snubby will love it too, I know he will. When will he come, Mr Martin?"

"I'll telephone your mother as soon as I can, and arrange for him to come tomorrow, if possible," said Mr Martin. "He can come by train to the nearest big town, and then get a taxi to bring him here. And let's hope Loony gets on all right with that goose – what's his name? – Waddle!"

"Well, what with Loony the spaniel, Miranda the monkey and Waddle the goose, we may have rather a hectic time," said Miss Pepper, with a laugh. "But I've coped with Snubby and Loony before, so I've no doubt I can manage."

"You go now? You go back home?" said Mrs Jones anxiously to Mr Martin. "You will not stay to have supper here, and taste the very good cooking?"

"No, I think not," said Mr Martin. "I'll go down and pick up the caravan and bring it up here, now that I know the others will be staying. Perhaps I could just have a cup of tea before I leave?"

"You shall, sir, yes, you shall have tea and good, buttery scones!" said Mrs Jones, and fled down the stairs as if she could smell the scones burning in the oven!

"Whew – what a non-stop talker!" said Roger. "We're going to have some very one-sided conversations, I can see!"

"I don't mind. I like her," said Diana. "She goes on and on like a babbling stream, but she's quite interesting. Oh, I am glad we're going to stay here. Sniff the air, Miss Pepper, isn't it clean and . . . and . . . mountainy? I wonder what Snubby will say – I'm sure he'll love it."

"Roger, you and Barney come down and help me with the caravan," said Mr Martin. "It may be a bit awkward getting it round those zigzaggy corners. You'd better walk behind and yell to me if I'm not giving it enough room to swing round."

"Okay," said the two boys, and went

down to the car with Mr Martin. They hopped in and went off to fetch the caravan. Miss Pepper and Diana took the opportunity of peeping into the other bedrooms. "They really look a bit like cells, with their stone walls and stone floors," said Diana. "Let's choose the one with the best views, Miss Pepper."

So they chose one with two windows, one window looking out over the sea, and the other into the mountains that rose one behind the other for miles. There were two small beds there, and the stone walls were partly draped with thick old curtains. A great chest stood against one wall, and Miss Pepper looked at it with interest.

"That must be pretty old," she said. "Our few belongings will be quite lost in there. And look at the ancient fireplace, Diana – you could almost put one of the beds in there!"

Diana went to the fireplace and put her head up the chimney. "I can see the sky!" she called. "It's a most enormous chimney!"

A voice spoke to them from the door. It was Mrs Jones, nodding and smiling. "I will show you a better room," she said. "This is not so comfortable as the others."

"But we love the view from here," said Miss Pepper, smiling. "And it looks really comfortable!"

"No. It is not the best room. Come, I will

show it to you." And she took Miss
Pepper's arm and led her to another room, a
little larger and better furnished. The view,
however, was not nearly so beautiful.

"No. I'd rather have the other room,"
said Miss Pepper firmly. "Because of the
view, you know."

Mrs Jones looked suddenly sulky. "I do
not like you to have that room," she said.
"It is not the best room. I will give you this
one."

But Miss Pepper was used to having her
own way, and shook her head with a polite
smile. "No, I have chosen the other room.
Now we will go down and see if Mr Martin

has the luggage!" And down they went to the great entrance, where Mr Martin and the boys were already waiting with the car and the caravan, having put the bags and suitcases down on the battered stone steps.

"What about my cup of tea?" said Mr Martin to Mrs Jones, smiling. "And then we'll just fix up terms, and I'll go!"

"Your tea – your beautiful scones!" cried Mrs Jones, rushing off down the dark passageway, presumably to the kitchen. "Wait one minute, sir, just one minute. The cooking here is . . ."

"Very good!" finished everyone at once, and Mr Martin chuckled. "What a woman! I should think she probably talks all night long in her sleep, wouldn't you?"

7

"Cooking Good! Very Good Cooking!"

When Mr Martin had gone, all the three children waving to him madly, and Miranda waving too, Roger put his hand over his tummy.

"Whew! What a tea Mrs Jones gave us! I never tasted such marvellous scones in my life! I had six!"

"Cooking good! Very good cooking!" quoted Diana. "Even Miranda had two scones. What's the time . . . just gone half past five, not too bad. What shall we do?"

"A little unpacking, please," said Miss Pepper promptly. "And a little arranging. I see that your father has put the caravan round the side of the inn, Barney, on that level piece. Is it safe there? There's such a slope down this hill."

"I'd better put heavy stones under the wheels," said Barney. "In case that small boy thinks up anything funny! He looks a bit of a monkey to me. Come and help me, Roger."

While the boys went to drag big stones to put under the wheels, Miss Pepper and Diana went upstairs to their room. They expected to find their luggage in the room with two windows that they had chosen, but it wasn't!

"Well! Don't tell me that Mrs Jones has put it in the best room that she kept trying to force on us!" said Miss Pepper crossly. "Go and look, Diana."

Diana went off to the best room, and came back at once. "Yes, it's there! What a nerve, really. She knew we said this one!"

"Well, we'll just go and get the suitcases and bring them here," said Miss Pepper, deciding that Mrs Jones must be kept firmly in her place, and do what her guests asked. So in half a minute the suitcases were in the room they had chosen, and were being unpacked. There were great drawers in the chest, and the clothes were hurriedly arranged inside.

In the middle of it there came a knock at their door. "Come in!" called Miss Pepper, in the briskest voice.

In came a tall man with thick, untidy hair, wearing glasses and a surly look. "Good evening," he said, "I am Mr Jones, the innkeeper. You have the wrong room. Please come this way to our best room."

"I've already chosen this one," said Miss Pepper. "It's quite empty and I prefer the view. You have no guest staying in it, I know."

"Madam, you will not like this room," said Mr Jones, looking even surlier.

"Please don't be so mysterious," said Miss Pepper, deciding that however well Mr Jones cooked, she was not going to like him. "Why shouldn't I like this room?"

"There are sometimes noises in the night," said Mr Jones solemnly.

"Oooh, how exciting! What kind of noises?" asked Diana. "Howls – yells – moans – or what?"

"You laugh," said Mr Jones angrily. "But you will not laugh in the middle of the night, when the noises come."

"Well, we'll see what they are like," said Miss Pepper, slamming the drawer of the chest shut. "Then we'll know whether to laugh or not. If you're trying to tell me the room's haunted or something, you're wasting your time. I don't believe in things like that."

Without another word Mr Jones walked out of the room. Miss Pepper looked at Diana. "Well, if I wasn't such an obstinate woman, I'd move out into the other room!" she said. "This is obviously a guest room, and I see no real reason why we shouldn't have it if we want it. Even the beds are made up and are all ready to sleep in!"

Soon all their clothes were stowed away

and they went down to see how the boys were getting on. Miss Pepper peeped into the caravan and was astonished and pleased to see everything put away so tidily.

As she stood there talking to the boys, the great grey goose came round the corner, cackling loudly. Behind it came the small, untidy boy, whistling.

He went right up to the caravan and had a good look inside. The goose looked in too, and made as if to climb in.

"Oh no you don't!" said Roger, and gave it a small push. "Geese not allowed in here!"

The goose hissed and flapped its wings. The boy put his arm round its neck, and it quietened down. He stared solemnly up at Roger with great dark eyes.

"What's your name?" said Diana, amused.

"Dafydd," said the boy.

"Oh – David," said Diana. "Come and look inside the caravan. Haven't you ever seen one before?"

Dafydd didn't understand what she was saying, but took her hand and went inside the caravan. He fingered everything with his dirty little hands, and finally took up a small comb from a hairbrush and slipped it into his pocket.

"No, no, Dafydd!" said Barney. "That's my comb, old son! Put it back!"

But Dafydd shook his head, and picked

60

up a tube of toothpaste. He examined it with interest. Then he suddenly felt something touching his pocket and looked down. It was Miranda, slipping a paw in, and taking out the comb! She was not going to allow anyone to steal Barney's belongings!

She leaped on to Barney's shoulder, chattering angrily, and began to comb his thick hair. Dafydd stared at her, frowning, rather scared. He said something in Welsh, something rather rude, and shook his little fist at Miranda, who immediately danced about on Barney's shoulder, saying plenty of rude things back to him in monkey-chatter.

"Cackle-cackle," said the goose outside, and flapped its wings impatiently. Miranda felt sure that it, too was saying something rude, and she leaped straight off Barney's shoulder down to the floor, and then, with another flying leap she was on the goose's back, clinging to its neck, chattering loudly.

The goose was so astonished that it fled at once, hissing like a dozen snakes, with Miranda riding it. Barney roared with laughter, and Dafydd at once battered him with his small fists, angry that anyone should make fun of his goose.

"Now, now," said Barney, holding Dafydd's small fists in one of his hands. "That's enough! The monkey won't hurt your Waddle. You go after him, and I'll call back the monkey. And listen – you're not to

come inside our caravan if we're not here.
Do you understand?"

Dafydd shouted something that nobody
could understand, kicked Barney on the
ankle, wrenched his hands away, and was
out of the caravan like a streak of lightning,
yelling for Waddle.

"Well – what do you think of that?" said
Barney to the others. "I vote we keep our
caravan locked when we're out anywhere.
What a little rascal!"

"His mother ought to keep him in order," said Miss Pepper. "Taking that comb right under our noses! We'd better keep our room locked too, Diana, when we're out. Ah, here comes Miranda. She's looking pleased with herself!"

Miranda did feel pleased with herself. She had put that flappy goose in its place! She had ridden on its back all the way to the cowshed a little way up the hill, the goose cackling at the top of its voice.

"Well, the goose will have to mind its p's and q's when Snubby comes with Loony," said Barney. "I can't see either of them putting up with Dafydd and Waddle for long, if they don't behave themselves."

"You two boys will be quite comfortable in the caravan at nights," said Miss Pepper. "The bunks are very good. Diana and I have got the room we wanted – the one with the heavenly view – though Mr Jones tried to scare us out of it with tales of noises in the night!"

"Oh, have you seen him?" said Barney. "He's not what you might call very merry and bright, is he? Roger and I thought he must have some secret sorrow, he looked so glum! But he's no right to try and scare you with tales of noises at night, Miss Pepper."

"Oh, he and his wife are proud of their best room, as they call it," said Miss Pepper. "He just hoped that a silly fib about noises would make us change rooms, that's all. I don't expect he has even noticed what wonderful views our room has!"

"Well, I don't mind noises, or pet geese or light-fingered small boys, so long as we get 'good cooking, very good cooking'!" said Diana. "We shall see what dinner's like."

Well, dinner was wonderful! Miss Pepper stared in amazement at the beautifully cooked meal. It began with chicken soup, went on to a fine joint of beef with mounds of roast potatoes, garden peas and the first runner beans, and finished with an ice-cream pudding set round with dainty biscuits of all kinds!

"I say! This is the best meal I've had since Dad took us out to a big hotel in London!" said Roger. "Look at the ice-cream pudding – there's enough for a dozen people. Are we supposed to eat it all, Miss Pepper?"

"Well, supposed to or not, I've no doubt you will!" said Miss Pepper, and they did! Miranda had the last little biscuit off the dish, and sat nibbling it on Barney's shoulder as Mrs Jones came in, beaming, to clear away.

"You like your supper?" she inquired, and laughed to hear the loud chorus that answered her.

"Cooking good, very good cooking!"

8

"Hello, Snubby!"

They were all sleepy after their wonderful meal, and they were yawning widely when Mrs Jones trotted in with a silver tray on which coffee cups were set.

"Dear me!" said Miss Pepper, surprised to see the gleaming silver and the steaming coffee. "Who would have thought that a little country inn like this would do everything so well! No wonder 'big people' sometimes come here, as Mrs Jones boasted! Coffee, anyone?"

"Anything to keep me awake!" said Barney, with a most tremendous yawn. "Miranda, that sugar is not for you. Smack her paw, Diana, please. She's as bad as that monkey of a Dafydd."

Far away, somewhere in the depths of the great dark hall, a bell shrilled. "The telephone!" said Miss Pepper. "I hope that's to say your aunt is getting on well, Diana."

Mrs Jones appeared. "Someone for you, Miss Pepper, please," she said, and out went

Miss Pepper, hoping for good news. She was soon back.

"That was your uncle," she said to Roger and Diana. "Barney's father got held up, and found he couldn't get back to your aunt's home tonight, so he telephoned your uncle and told him to send Snubby off to us by train early tomorrow. Snubby is absolutely too excited for words, he said, and Loony promptly went mad!"

Everyone laughed. Roger rubbed his hands together. "Good old Snubby! Funny we should be so pleased to have such a pest with us, but things always seem to happen when Snubby and Loony are around. What time will he arrive?"

"Probably by the half past twelve train, at Dilcarmock, five miles from here," said Miss Pepper. "I'll telephone to order a taxi to meet him and bring him here. Your aunt is going on well, so your uncle sounded quite happy."

"He'll feel even happier tomorrow when he's got rid of Snubby," said Roger. "Last time he stayed there Snubby kept pretending to have a banjo and made banjo noises all day long. Uncle and Aunt nearly went crazy!"

Miss Pepper groaned, remembering the holiday at Rubabdub when Snubby had imagined himself playing all kinds of instruments, not only banjos. "I only hope he doesn't take it into his head to have a banjo here," she said. "Anyone want any more coffee?"

Nobody did. One by one they yawned again, and Miss Pepper laughed. "Let's all go to bed," she said. "It's well past nine o'clock and we've had a very long day. Off to the caravan, boys – and sleep well! See you at breakfast time. It's at half past eight, so if any one wants an early morning swim, there'll be plenty of time."

"Right. I'm half asleep already," said Roger, getting up. He gave Miss Pepper a sudden hug that surprised her. "I think you're really great to stay on with us like this after our caravan holiday broke up!" he said. "I hope to goodness you don't hear any unpleasant noises in the night!"

"Well, we'll lean out of one of our windows and yell if we do!" said Miss Pepper, pleased at the sudden hug.

"This will be your last peaceful night, boys," said Diana, with a grin. "Tomorrow you'll have Snubby in the caravan with you, and mad-dog Loony!"

The boys left, and Miss Pepper and Diana went upstairs, meeting Mrs Jones on the way. "A truly wonderful meal, Mrs Jones," said Miss Pepper. "Your husband is surely a trained chef?"

"Oh, yes indeed," said Mrs Jones proudly. "It was in London that he was trained, Miss

Pepper, at a big, important hotel. We were so happy there. I was a chambermaid, and he was second chef. I wanted to stay – but no, Mr Jones he wanted to come back here, where he was born. His cooking is good, very good!"

Miss Pepper nodded, said goodnight and went on up the stairs, half wondering whether she would find their things removed from their room-with-a-view to the best room. But no – their cases were still in the room they had chosen. Good! Miss Pepper was also pleased to see that there was a key in the door.

"Now we can lock our room when we leave it," she said to Diana, "and be sure that that monkey of a Dafydd won't come in with his cackling goose and pocket whatever takes his fancy!"

She and Diana were soon in bed and fast asleep. Were there any noises in the night? There might well have been, even if only the wind in the chimney, but neither of them would have heard a thunderstorm that night! The beds were so comfortable, the room was airy, and they slept so soundly that they only awoke when Mrs Jones came knocking at their door with cups of tea.

Breakfast was as good as dinner had been. Cold ham, boiled eggs, hot toast, homemade marmalade, creamy butter, and scalding hot coffee . . . Miss Pepper looked at the table with much approval.

"Snubby will like this place," said Roger, taking his second boiled egg. "Have you phoned about a taxi for him yet, Miss Pepper?"

"No, there's time enough after breakfast," said Miss Pepper. "Did you and Barney swim? I should imagine you did by your appetites!"

"Well, we didn't!" said Roger, with a grin. "We slept like logs – and I don't think we'd have wakened when we did if that young Dafydd hadn't come peering in at the caravan window and wakened up Miranda. She leaped out of the window and chased Waddle the goose all over the place, and what with Dafydd's yells and the goose's cackles, we woke up with an awful jump! Why doesn't somebody scold Dafydd?"

"Someone's going to, if he doesn't look out," said Barney grimly, rubbing his hands together.

Miss Pepper went out to phone for a taxi for Snubby. "I've ordered one to call here at half past eleven," she said. "I thought you three would like to go in it to meet Snubby. It's the only one in the village, apparently, so it's probably a poor old crock."

"Right," said Barney, pleased at the idea of meeting Snubby at the station. "We'll have time to go down for a swim, then. Are you all coming? Merlin's Cove is supposed to be the best swimming place, apparently."

Mrs Jones agreed that it was indeed the best place when she came in to clear away the breakfast. Dafydd and Waddle also came in with her, and Waddle immediately pecked at a piece of toast left on one of the plates. Mrs Jones didn't say a word of reproof – but Miranda did! She snatched the toast out of the goose's beak, and then pulled her tail feathers hard, chattering angrily all the time.

Dafydd aimed a blow at the monkey, and Barney was immediately beside him, holding his hands tightly.

"No! Do you want to be bitten? Miranda has very sharp teeth. I will show you them.

Come here, Miranda." Dafydd stared at the monkey's sharp teeth and turned away, gabbling in Welsh.

"He says your monkey must not hurt his goose," said Mrs Jones, clearing away. "Dafydd, go away. You are not to come in here now that we have visitors. Take Waddle with you."

Dafydd went out sulkily, Waddle following behind. "Waddle was just a little gosling when Dafydd had him," said Mrs Jones. "He broke his leg and Dafydd mended it – he put a stick, like so, and tied it well. And Waddle's leg mended, and now he will not leave Dafydd, and what a trouble those two are, I give you my word, and what is the use of my scolding him, he hears only what he wants to hear, he does only what he—"

It looked as if Mrs Jones was launched on one of her never-ending speeches, and Miss Pepper interrupted her firmly.

"We would rather that Dafydd and Waddle did not come into the dining-room or into our bedroom," she said.

"But how can I stop them?" argued Mrs Jones, deftly folding up the tablecloth. "They go where they please, they—"

"Not while we're here!" said Miss Pepper. "Er – have you ever tried a good scolding, Mrs Jones?"

"A scolding! A scolding is no good with that one!" said Mrs Jones. "Even if you could catch him! Like an eel he is, like a slippery eel, and as for Waddle, he is as bad, the way he walks where he wants to walk, and cackles when he wants to cackle, and . . ."

But there was no one to listen to her! The room was empty, the boys had slipped out to swim, Diana had gone too, and Miss Pepper had hurried quietly out of the room! Mrs Jones went on talking for a long time before she saw she was alone – and even then she didn't stop, but talked away to herself as she carried out the tray to the kitchen.

The boys couldn't find their swimming things, and there was a great to-do at once. "Miss Pepper! Miss Pepper! Ask Di if she's got our things with her, will you?" shouted Barney, as he saw Miss Pepper at her bedroom window. "Ours aren't in the caravan, that's certain."

Diana hunted hurriedly in the drawer where she had put her clothes, and at last found the boys' swimming trunks. She threw them out of the window, and one pair caught on a rambler growing up the wall.

"Ass!" shouted Roger. "Now I'll have to get a ladder. Why on earth can't girls throw properly!"

"Oh dear – if you don't hurry up the taxi will be here," said Miss Pepper, looking at her watch. She called down to the boys. "I don't think you'd better swim after all – you'll miss Snubby's train if you do!"

And then, what a surprise! A piercing, very well-known voice came to their startled ears – surely, surely, it couldn't be Snubby's?

"Hello, everybody! Here I am!"

And someone came up the slope to the inn – someone very dirty indeed, with straw sticking out of him at every corner and a black dog careering at his heels.

"Snubby! We were just going to meet you!" yelled Roger. "How did you get here? Your train isn't even due in yet. How awful you look! What in the world have you been doing?"

9

Hot Bath for Snubby!

Snubby marched up to the astonished Roger and Barney, grinning all over his freckled, snub-nosed face. His ginger hair was very wind-blown indeed!

Diana and Miss Pepper ran downstairs, most amazed. How like Snubby to arrive so unexpectedly!

"Have I given you a surprise?" he said. "I thought I should!"

"Snubby – how did you get here so soon? And why are you so filthy?" said Miss Pepper. "Hello, Loony – good gracious, you're all covered in straw too!"

"Well, Uncle got me a ticket for an awful slow train," said Snubby, rubbing his dirty face with an even dirtier handkerchief. "And I heard there was a very early one, so I decided to catch that. You see, Uncle was getting pretty fed up with me, really. I arrived at Dilcarmock ages ago, and I got a lift in a trailer that was loaded with straw and stuff for Penrhyndendraith, or whatever this place is called. Gosh, it crawled, though, and the straw was frightfully prickly."

"Snubby, you look too awful for words," said Diana. "Honestly, I've never seen such a tramp!"

"Well, I did think you'd all be more pleased to see me," said Snubby, sounding hurt. "I tell you, I couldn't stay with Uncle any longer. He just glowered at me till I almost changed into a worm. Darling Miranda, are you pleased to see me?"

The little monkey leaped on to his shoulder and put her tiny paws down his neck, chattering softly. Yes – she was very pleased to see Snubby – and Loony too!

Loony was tearing all round the place, sniffing into every corner. He had given everyone a really good lick, and was now interested in all the new smells. And then, quite suddenly, he saw a most fearsome creature coming towards him, hissing like a dozen snakes!

It was Waddle, of course. Waddle, who detested dogs and cats – and monkeys! Waddle considered that the inn belonged to him and to no one else, and woe betide any strange creature who dared to sniff around his domain!

Loony took one look at Waddle and backed away hurriedly. What in the world was this creature? Bird? Animal? Snake? Its head and neck and voice seemed to be those of a snake – but it had wings!

Loony let out a terrified yelp and ran to Snubby.

"Don't be an ass, Loony, it's only a goose!" said Snubby – and then promptly ran for shelter himself as Waddle cackling, hissing and flapping, descended upon him and Loony too!

But little Miranda was not going to have her friends scattered like this, and entered into the battle with delight! She flung herself on Waddle's back and clasped his neck as she had done once before, chattering at the top of her voice.

Then it was Waddle's turn to run, and off went the goose into the house, waddling more quickly than ever a goose waddled before, cackling as if the house was on fire! Miranda clung to him tightly, and the goose could not shake her off.

Loony recovered his courage and raced after them, barking madly. Mr Jones, coming to see what the noise was about, met the goose and Miranda with Loony immediately behind them, and was promptly bowled over. He sat down very suddenly indeed, knocked over by the heavy goose, and then trodden on by the surprised Loony.

Miss Pepper put her hands to her face, and groaned. Why did things like this always happen when Snubby was around? He had only to appear, and the whole world seemed at once to go crazy. And now there was Mr Jones, tall and thin and dour, getting up from the stone hall floor, rubbing himself angrily.

"Oh, Mr Jones, I hope you're not hurt," said Miss Pepper, hurrying to him. "The goose frightened the dog, and then the monkey frightened the goose, and the dog ran after them both, and, and . . ."

"And the cow jumped over the moon," said Snubby with a hoot of laughter.

Mr Jones took one look at him and raised his voice. "Get out of here, you dirty

little tramp! Go where you belong, into the gutter! Don't dare come up to this inn, where decent folk stay!"

There was a surprised silence, while everyone stared first at Mr Jones, and then at Snubby. Snubby glanced down at his dirty clothes apologetically, and then looked beseechingly at Miss Pepper.

"Er – this is a cousin of Roger and Diana Lynton," said Miss Pepper. "The one whom Mr Martin arranged to come and stay, you remember. He's had a long – and – er – a very dirty journey. He needs a – a wash."

Mr Jones glared at them all, and limped back down the hall without a word. Miss Pepper took hold of Snubby.

"You're going to have a hot bath," she said. "And I'm going to scrub you from head to foot – you – you dirty little tramp! Really, Snubby, I cannot imagine how anyone can get as filthy as you look."

"Where's that goose gone?" said Snubby, pretending not to hear. "I can't stop old Loony from going for him if he appears again."

"Don't worry about Loony – he'll retire into the darkest corner he can find, if he sees Waddle," said Miss Pepper, keeping a firm hold of Snubby and propelling him towards the hall door. "Thank goodness the creature has disappeared and Miranda's recovered herself. I do wish you'd caught the proper train, Snubby, and not caused all this sensation! We don't want to be turned out of this place. The cooking is so—"

"Very, very good!" finished Barney, with a grin. He put his arm round Snubby's shoulder. "Cheer up! Where's your luggage? Get out your trunks and come and swim with us – you'll soon be clean then."

"No," said Miss Pepper at once. "I don't see why he should make the sea absolutely black! Is that all the luggage you've got, Snubby – that small case there? My goodness – you can't have much in it!"

"Well, I thought Roger could lend me what I've forgotten," said Snubby amiably, going indoors with Miss Pepper. "Gosh, I feel a bit tired now. Come on, Loony. Is there anything to eat, Miss Pepper? I do feel awfully empty. I say, what a place this is! I thought it was a ruin, till the farmer told me it was the inn I'd asked him to drop me at. I say, I do hope I'm going to sleep in the caravan with the others, I—"

"Snubby! Stop talking for a minute," said Miss Pepper, quite fiercely. "I want to see if you can have a bath. Stay here while I go to the kitchen. Don't dare to move from there, because if Mr Jones sees you again he might quite well pick you up and throw you into the sea – and I wouldn't blame him either!"

"I say – you are peppery this morning, Miss Pepper darling!" said Snubby, taken by surprise. "And I'd so looked forward to seeing you again, too. I never . . ."

But Miss Pepper was gone, walking quickly down the dark hallway to the equally dark kitchen, which was huge and rather forbidding. Mrs Jones was there, doing some washing-up in an enormous sink.

"Oh, Mrs Jones – do you think I might run a bath?" asked Miss Pepper. "The children's cousin has arrived and he's really very dirty."

"Yes, of course, most certainly," said Mrs Jones.

Miss Pepper, thankful that Mrs Jones did not chatter on and on as she usually did, went to collect Snubby, determined that he should not escape her.

"You dirty little ragamuffin!" she said as she saw him patiently waiting for her on exactly the same spot where she had left him, Loony sitting beside him. "You look as if you've just been sweeping a chimney! I never did know anyone who could—"

"Get dirty wherever he goes and whatever he does," finished Snubby with a grin. "I wonder how many times you've said that to each of us, Miss Pepper! Where's the bathroom?"

It wasn't long before Snubby was clean and shining all over, even to the backs of his ears. It wasn't any good protesting that he could wash himself, Miss Pepper was determined to get him really clean. Loony sat beside the bath, watching in alarm, half-afraid that it might be his turn next!

"Now dry yourself, and I'll go and find something for you to eat," said Miss Pepper. "Look at the bath water – what a disgrace! It will take you quite a bit of time to clean the bath!"

Snubby sighed. He thought it was very hard that no matter what he did, he got into trouble. He rubbed himself dry and talked to the listening Loony.

"She called me a ragamuffin! What do you think of that, Loony? Except that it sounds like something to eat, it's a horrid name to give anyone. Ragamuffin! Now what am I supposed to put on? Those clean clothes, I suppose – my own tee-shirt, Roger's old shorts and this looks like Barney's shirt, it's so big! Loony, you don't know how lucky you are to be born a dog, and be able to wear the same fur coat all your life. Like to try this shirt on, old thing?"

Loony retreated to the door at once, and scratched at it, whining, suddenly afraid that it might enter Snubby's head to pop him into the bath.

"I'm not ready yet, old chap," said Snubby, looking down into the bath, where the dirty water had already left a black line all round the sides. "I say, Loony – come and look at this! I've got to clean this bath, and it will take me ages!"

Loony put his paws up on the side of the bath and looked down at the water, wagging his tail. He didn't mind looking, so long as he wasn't going to be bathed in it. He couldn't imagine why anyone ever had baths. Snubby suddenly sniffed, and bent down over Loony. "You know, you smell pretty awful," he said. "I've a good mind to pop you in too, and—"

But very fortunately for the scared Loony, Miss Pepper's voice suddenly sounded outside the door.

"Snubby! What in the world are you doing? Aren't you dressed yet? I hope you've cleaned the bath. There is a piece of meat-pie and some bread and cheese downstairs, if you hurry!"

Snubby hurried at once. He let out the bath water and hurriedly tried to remove the black line round the bath with the flannel Miss Pepper had given him, finished dressing, and grinned at Loony as he opened the bathroom door. "Loony – I have a feeling we'll enjoy being here. We're going to have quite an exciting time!"

Well, Snubby, you're right. But perhaps it will be rather *too* exciting!

10

Snubby Gets Into Trouble

Snubby thoroughly enjoyed his first day at Penrhyndendraith, and so did the others. They went swimming that sunny morning, and found Merlin's Cove. It was a truly lovely place.

The sands were almost white there, and as smooth as silk to walk on. When the tide was up it swept right into all the caves that made up Merlin's Cove. These ran either a little way or a long way into the high rocky cliff, and two were labelled DANGEROUS.

"Ha – let's see why they're dangerous," said Snubby, peering into one, and was at once firmly taken by the arm by Barney.

"Any fatheadedness on your part and you go straight back to another of your aunts and uncles," he said. "Do you want rocks falling on your head – or to lose your way for ever in a maze of cliff tunnels? Aren't you ever going to grow up, Snubby?"

Loony ran a little way into the dark, low cave, and then turned his head as if to say

"Come on, Snubby!" but Snubby yelled to him to come back at once.

"Come back, ass! Aren't you ever going to grow up?"

They explored some of the other caves, and found most of them shallow, going back only a little way. They swam twice, and lay in the sun. Miranda hated the water and wouldn't go near it, though Barney at last persuaded her to paddle, and held her paw like a child.

Loony splashed past her and once out of his depth and swimming, turned his head as if to say "Monkeys are poor creatures! They can only paddle!"

"It looks as if we're going to have a pretty good time here," said Roger, lying on the sand, leaning on his elbow. "Look – are those fishing-boats coming in? Aren't they lovely?"

They were! They all had brown sails of different shades, and came in smoothly on the wind, the tide taking them to the little jetty not far off. The children scrambled up to go and see the catch. Miranda waited till Loony had come out of the water, and was vigorously shaking himself, and then leaped straight on to his back, clinging there with all her might, jigging up and down as if wanting a ride. This was an old trick of Miranda's, and one that Loony didn't approve of at all! He set off at top speed, hoping the little monkey would be bumped off, but she clung on for dear life, winding her tail round his tummy.

"Loony, roll over on the sand, you idiot!" shouted Snubby. "Have you forgotten how to get her off?"

Loony promptly rolled over and Miranda had to leap off, scampering to Barney quickly before Loony could catch her. The children laughed, and ran over to the jetty. They watched the great catch of fish being emptied. There were some large crabs among the catch and Miranda was most interested in them as they began to walk off sideways. She tapped one, and almost had her paw caught by one of its big claws! After that she and Loony kept well away from the crawling crabs.

They were all very hungry by lunch-time, and went back through the little straggling village and up the slope of the hill to the old inn. They passed the ice cream shop, and Snubby at once wanted to go in and buy ice creams when he heard how the others had sampled them the day before.

"No, you'll spoil your lunch," said Barney. "Do come on. I feel quite hollow inside with hunger."

Miss Pepper had had a peaceful morning, except for twenty minutes when Mrs Jones saw her wandering round the old garden of the inn, and came out to talk non-stop.

Miss Pepper made up her mind that she would rather go down to the beach with the children than risk being found by Mrs Jones again!

It really was a very pleasant first day, marred only by an accident to Snubby's clothes – or rather to the shirt and the shorts which belonged to Barney and Roger.

Barney suddenly saw that his nice shirt, which had been almost new, was torn right down the back. He felt very cross.

"What on earth have you done to ruin my shirt like that?" he demanded. "It's my newest one – I've hardly worn it myself! I didn't mind lending it to you till you had your own clothes sent on, but I do think you might have been more careful with it! And look at Roger's shorts! Have you sat down in a patch of oil or something? You are in a filthy mess!"

Snubby tried to screw himself round to see the shorts. "I wondered what that horrible smell was that seemed to follow me around," he said. "Well I never! When could I have sat in oil? I'm awfully sorry, Roger – and sorry about your shirt too, Barney."

"Well, I don't know what you're going to do tomorrow for clothes," said Roger. "Borrow a skirt of Diana's, I suppose! I'm certainly not going to lend you any more of my things."

Miss Pepper was also very annoyed, and stared in horror as Snubby presented himself to her and asked her advice about the oil.

"To think I scrubbed you from head to toe this morning – and you look exactly like a ragamuffin again!" she said. "Well, you'll have to stay in bed tomorrow while I wash your own dirty clothes, the ones you took off this morning."

"Oh, no!" cried Snubby in horror. "Stay in bed? I couldn't!"

But Miss Pepper was quite firm about that and the next day Snubby found himself compelled to have his breakfast in the caravan, sitting in his bunk. He was very angry indeed, and Loony simply couldn't understand what all the fuss was about.

"I simply daren't borrow anything else of Barney's or Roger's," groaned Snubby to a sympathetic Loony. "And as I've only got my old tee-shirt to wear, or my pyjamas, I don't see how I can go out of the caravan till Miss Pepper cleans up those torn, dirty things of mine."

He lay and thought angry thoughts for a time, and then an idea came into his head. "That ice cream shop!" he said. "I believe it sells second-hand clothes. I'm sure I saw some hanging up. Loony, what about us slipping out and buying some before the others come back? I'm *not* going to lie here all day! I'll turn my pyjama trousers up to

my knees so that they're more like shorts, and keep this tee-shirt on."

And, very soon, a rather peculiar figure slipped out of the caravan and ran down to the little village. Snubby grinned as he looked down at himself, and wondered whether the old lady in the shop would notice his peculiar attire.

Old Mrs Jones, her snow-white hair tucked under the black net cap, didn't seem at all surprised to see a small boy in tee-shirt and turned-up pyjama legs.

"You'll be one of the children up at the inn?" she said in her singsong voice, with a twinkle in her eye. "Is it an ice cream you are wanting to buy?"

"Well, yes – among other things," said

Snubby, giving her the grin that always made old ladies love him. "Look – I've got into trouble over my clothes, and I want to buy some more. Have you got any that would fit me – second-hand ones I mean?"

"Well, now, there's a pair of trousers," said old Mrs Jones, pointing to a most dilapidated pair, hanging on a hook. "Clean they are, though dirty they look, for I washed them myself. And there's this tee-shirt, red and yellow, colourful it is, and not badly worn."

"Trousers would be fine," said Snubby, pleased, and put them on over his pyjama legs. "Hey, Loony, how do I look?"

Lonny barked sharply and wagged his tail. "He says I look about sixteen, instead of twelve," said Snubby with a grin. "Now for the tee-shirt – my word, I've gone bright haven't I! Is it clean? Because if it isn't, Miss Pepper will rip it off me at once!"

"It is clean," said Mrs Jones. "And you shall have a cap too – a good one. See the big peak!"

Snubby put it on and fancied himself very much in it. "Thanks awfully," he said. "How much do I owe you?"

"That will be a pound for the lot – and an ice cream thrown in for nothing," said Mrs Jones, laughing at Snubby's peculiar appearance.

"Oh, I say – that's very kind of you,"

said Snubby, and paid up at once. He took the ice-cream cornet gratefully.

"It is my son who has the inn where you are staying," said Mrs Jones. "So good he is at cooking! He went to London to learn. Ah, to think that a poor boy like my Llewellyn, with never two pairs of trousers to his name, should have gone to London and learned to cook! And now that inn is his! Always, all his life, he has said to me, 'Ah, if only that inn was mine!' How I laughed! 'I have fifty pounds in my old tea caddy,' I said, 'and that has taken me eighteen years to save – and you want to own that inn'!"

"Gosh – how did he get it then?" asked Snubby, licking the last of the ice cream.

"He made friends in London," the old lady said proudly. "Important friends. And they lent him the money to buy the inn he so much wanted. How happy my Llewellyn is now!"

Snubby thought of the cross-looking, dour man he had seen the night before. "Goodness – he doesn't look very happy!" he said. "I say! I must go! Miss Pepper will be sending out a search party for me or something. Goodbye and many thanks!"

And away he rushed, really a very peculiar figure indeed. What in the world would the others say?

11

A Very Strange Happening

Snubby had a few moments of doubt as he
walked up the steep slope to the inn. "If
they jeer at me I shall run away!" he said to
Loony, who wagged his tail sympathetically.

The first person he met was the boy
Daffyd, with his faithful goose. Dafydd gave
a loud shriek when he saw him and tore off
with Waddle behind him – though whether
the shriek was because Snubby looked so
peculiar or because he was scared of Loony
was not clear. Snubby stared after him,
frowning. If that was the effect he was
going to have, things were not going to be
easy!

Roger, Diana and Barney came out of the
inn at that moment. They had been looking
everywhere for Snubby, having missed him
from the caravan. They looked at him, not
recognising him in the least, and wondered
why Loony was following this peculiar-
looking lad.

Snubby had pulled the big peaked cap

down over his face, and he grinned when he saw that the others did not recognise him. He swaggered up to them, hands in pockets, and pretended to speak in Welsh, in a peculiar-sounding hoarse voice.

"Collq-inna-dooly-hector-sonkin-poppyll?" he said, his cap still pulled down over his face.

"What on earth is this fellow saying?" asked Roger, astonished. "And why is Loony with him?"

Diana gave a sudden shriek, and pulled at Snubby's cap. "It's Snubby! *Snubby!* Where have you been? Where did you get those awful clothes?"

"They're not awful. They're fine – and clean," said Snubby, turning himself round and round so that they could admire him. "I bought them at the ice cream shop – second-hand."

"Snubby! How could you buy clothes like that – you don't know who's worn them before!" said Roger.

"What does it matter? I tell you, they're clean!" roared Snubby. "Oh goodness gracious – here comes Miss Pepper!"

What the others had said was nothing to what Miss Pepper said! She insisted that he should go straight back to the caravan and take off "those terrible clothes, especially that cap," and wait till she came with clean ones.

"I'm not going to," said Snubby obstinately. "Fancy expecting me to waste a lovely morning like this in that caravan, when I've gone and got myself clothes to wear. It's no good, Miss Pepper, I'm going to wear these clothes till my others are clean – and if you all think I'm not fit company for you, all right, Loony and I will keep away from you! Come on, Loony – they're looking at us as if we were a couple of bad smells!"

And with that Snubby marched very quickly off down the hill, his peaked cap at a very cheeky angle indeed. Diana called crossly after him. "Well – you *do* smell in those clothes! You smell dreadful!"

Snubby took no notice at all, and soon disappeared round a bend. Miss Pepper suddenly began to laugh.

"Oh dear!" she said. "What a sight he looks – and yet I really do believe he's quite proud of those awful clothes. I only hope to goodness he won't want to go on wearing them when his own are ready. Well – what are you three going to do today?"

"Swim – have a walk, perhaps fish if we can get a boat," said Barney. "It's a pity Snubby's behaving like this. Why didn't he think of putting on his swimming things – it's warm enough for him to wear them all day long on the beach. I'll take them down with me, shall I? – in case he does join us, and then I can tell him to wear them, and stay with us."

So when the others went down to the beach, they took Snubby's swimming things with them. But there was no sign of him, or of Loony either!

Snubby was angry and hurt. Fancy calling him a bad smell! He caught sight of himself in the glass window of the ice cream shop as he went by, and stopped. Hm! He did look a bit odd, perhaps. Pity the trousers were so big and sloppy and the tee-shirt *was* certainly a bit loud. But the cap was fine!

"I suppose we look a bit ragamuffinish again, Loony," he said sorrowfully. "Now – what shall we do? I know – we'll find a nice quiet place, and read that code letter from old Bruce. I'll tell you what he says."

Loony wagged his tail. He knew who Bruce was – a very close school-friend of Snubby's, a rascal almost as bad as Snubby, the bane of their form-master. The two of them had invented a most involved secret code, using both figures and letters. It took Snubby about two hours to write a letter in their secret code – and even longer to decipher any he got from Bruce! Still, it made them both feel very important indeed, and they enjoyed that.

"We'll go somewhere out of sight of the others," said Snubby to Loony. "Look – what about going down to that broken bit of cliff over there – see? We could hide among the fallen rocks and see what old Bruce has got to say in his letter."

So down they went together and were soon ensconced among the warm rocks, the sea not very far away. Snubby took out Bruce's letter. It was on a squared piece of paper, neatly torn out of his maths book.

Snubby looked at it and gave a small groan. "It's rather a long one," he said to Loony, gazing at the mass of neat little figures, interspersed with letters. "It'll take us ages to decode. Still, it's all good practice, Loony. You never know when you might have to use a code. Now – let's see – 12 – 6 – J – 567 – P – gosh, what does P stand for now? I wish I had my code-book with me. Hello – who's this?"

A man was coming over the rocks towards them. He was short, with a black beard, and wore dark sunglasses. Snubby glanced up at him, expecting him to pass by. But he didn't.

He came towards Snubby, and stood beside him. "Give that to me!" he said in an angry voice.

Snubby was extremely startled. He hastily stuffed his precious code letter in to his pocket. "What's up?" he said. "What do you want?"

"That letter!" said the man savagely. "How dare you open it and read it?"

"Well, why shouldn't I? It was sent to me, not to you," said Snubby, beginning to feel that the man must be crazy. "Don't be daft!"

"You know you had to meet me here and give me that letter," said the man, his voice shaking with rage. "And I find you have opened it and are trying to decipher it! How dare you! I shall see that your uncle punishes you well!"

"What on earth are you talking about?" said Snubby, absolutely at sea. "This is *not* your letter. It's mine, and I'm certainly not going to give it to you. It's in a very secret code that my friend and I know."

"Your friend? Your friend knows the code – and you too? You lie!" said the man. "You are a foolish boy who hopes to make me give you money for handing over my letter."

"Oh, don't be an ass," said Snubby, getting up. "If this is a joke, it's pretty silly. I'm going!"

But to his enormous surprise the man threw him roughly back on the rocks, dug his hand into Snubby's pocket and tore out the letter. This was too much for Loony! He began to growl angrily. With a very fierce snarl Loony flung himself on the surprised man, who shook him off with great force. He picked up a piece of rock and flung it at Loony, who only just dodged in time.

"Loony! Come here! He'll kill you!" shouted Snubby. "He's absolutely mad. Let him go."

Reluctantly Loony sat down and watched the bearded man clamber up the cliff and on to the roadway. The little spaniel growled angrily till he was out of sight, sad that he could not chase him. He turned to Snubby and whimpered, pawing him as if to say "Are you hurt? Is everything all right?"

"I'm not hurt, only angry," said Snubby, "and very puzzled too. Why did he come here to me? Did he think I was someone else? And what on earth was he gassing on about – a letter in code, he said, and took my letter from old Bruce! I suppose he saw it was in code. Look here, Loony, there's something peculiar about this. Let's go and find the others."

And off they went along the beach. They soon saw the others sitting on the sands, sunning themselves after a swim. Snubby went up to them and sat down.

"Got something to tell you all," he said in a low, mysterious voice. "Listen!"

At once they sat up, grinning at Snubby's peculiar appearance, but eager to hear him. He began to relate what had happened.

They all listened, quite astonished. Barney whistled. "You're not making this up by any chance, are you?" he said, for Snubby had at times invented some curious stories.

"No! No, of course I'm not," said Snubby indignantly. "It's true, every word of it – and here's the bruise I got on my elbow when that fellow flung me down on the rocks."

He showed them quite a massive bruise. Barney looked at it and frowned.

"Either that fellow's quite mad – or there's something extraordinary going on," he said. "Why did he mistake you for someone else, though? You must have looked like the person he was to meet – a real tramp, if you don't mind my saying so, Snubby. A proper ragamuffin! The kind of person who might be a go-between, if something dirty was going on."

"I'll take these things off at once then," said Snubby hastily. "Got my swimming things? I'll just pop behind that rock. A go-between! Phew – just wait till I see the real one, if I ever do!" He went behind a rock and hastily flung off his awful clothes, putting on a pair of swimming trunks. And then, just as he joined the others, someone passed them, dressed in clothes very like Snubby's – long, dirty-looking trousers, a bright stripy tee-shirt, a peaked cap – and behind him ran a small black dog!

"There you are!" whispered Barney, nudging Snubby very hard indeed. "See! I bet that's the fellow you were mistaken for – a regular ragamuffin! He's even got a little black dog – a poodle cross I should think – and he's making for the rocks over there where you were sitting. Now what do we do?"

12

Snubby and the Ragamuffin

They all watched the little ragamuffin go to the patch of fallen rocks where Snubby had sat. The small dog leaped about at his heels, and then sat down by him, as he settled himself on one of the rocks.

"See? He's waiting for someone," said Roger. "I bet he's got the real secret code-letter all right – the one that mad fellow thought you had!"

"I expect that man was told to look out for a ragamuffin of a boy, sitting on those rocks, with a black dog," said Barney. "And the boy would hand him a letter – secret instructions about something or other, I should think, and—"

"And old Snubby happened to go to that very spot, looking like a ragamuffin himself – with Loony who's as black as any dog can be expected to be!" said Roger. "And what's more, Snubby happened to be reading a letter in code – his code and Bruce's – but how was the man to know that? He must have been certain it was his own code letter!"

"Gosh – no wonder he was furious with me then!" said Snubby. "He must have thought I was actually trying to decipher his secret instructions, or whatever they were! You know, he might have killed Loony, if that rock he threw had hit him!"

"I think this is pretty serious," said Barney. "Do we tell Miss Pepper, or not?"

"We don't!" said Diana, at once. "She might want to leave immediately! And it is so nice here! I don't expect anything horrible will happen now, especially as Snubby has taken off those frightful clothes. You're not to wear them again, Snubby."

"Not even the cap?" said Snubby, disappointed. "I rather fancied myself in that."

"Certainly not the cap," said Barney. He stared round at the boy still sitting patiently on the fallen rocks some way along the beach. "That kid will have to sit there a long time! The bearded fellow won't be back, that's certain. He's probably going slowly mad trying to decipher Snubby's code, and making it fit in with his!"

"I'm going to talk to that boy," said Snubby, getting up. "I might find out something about my letter."

"Better not," said Roger.

"Why?" said Snubby, walking off in his swimming things. "We're sure that horrible fellow with the beard won't come back again – he thinks he's got the letter he wanted. The boy will think I'm just some tripper or other."

And off he went with Loony, whistling a tune, jigging along in time to it. When he came near to the waiting boy, he suddenly remembered his musician pretence, and began to make a noise like a banjo, pretending to strum with his fingers.

It was a very peculiar noise and the boy looked up at once, thinking he was hearing a real banjo. He was astonished to see Snubby's pretence, and laughed.

Twang-a-twang-a-twang-a-twang-a-twang – twang-a-twang-twang! The sounds that Snubby made between his teeth were exactly like a cheap banjo!

"Hello!" he said, sitting down grinning, "I like your little dog. What's his name?"

"Woolly," said the boy, running his hand over the poodle's woolly back. "What's your dog's name?"

"Loony," said Snubby. "Short for lunatic. You waiting for someone?"

"Yes. A man with a beard," said the boy. "Got to give him a letter from my uncle."

"Who's your uncle?" said Snubby, strumming his pretend banjo again.

"Morgan," said the boy, beginning to imitate Snubby. *Twang-a-twang-a-twang!* "He was a fisherman, but he broke his leg – and he lets out fishing boats now instead of fishing."

"Why didn't he post the letter?" said Snubby. "Lazy fellow!"

"How do I know?" said the boy. "I say, look at your dog and mine making friends! I do wish that man would come for his letter. I thought I was late – but he's later still. And I did want to go out in a boat with my pa this morning."

"All right. You give me the letter and I'll wait here for him," said Snubby. "And if he comes I'll give it to him, see? He won't know I'm not you, will he – we've both got a black dog!"

"Well – I'd get a fine telling-off if anyone found out," said the boy. "But I'm not waiting here all morning. Here, take the letter and wait till he comes. Don't say a word about me, though!"

"Right. You go off," said Snubby, feeling suddenly very excited. "I'll wait about on these rocks with Loony, my own black dog!"

The boy thrust an envelope into Snubby's hands and went off quickly, his poodle at his heels. Snubby sat there on the rocks, and waited, his heart beating. The man wouldn't come back, of course – but he must stay here on the rocks till the boy was out of sight!

It seemed ages till the boy disappeared.

Snubby looked along the beach, to where he had left the others. They were all there, watching intently.

Snubby stood up as soon as the boy was out of sight, and then he and Loony raced over the sands to the other three. He flung himself down beside them, panting.

"The boy *was* waiting for a man with a beard," he said. "His uncle – a man called Morgan, who hires out boats – gave the letter to him to deliver. The boy didn't say why – I don't think he knew. He's a bit slow, I think. He said he was late, and he hoped the man would come soon because he wanted to go out in a boat with his father."

"And so you offered to wait in his place and deliver the letter?" said Barney. "We wondered what was happening when the boy suddenly went off."

"Yes. And he gave me the letter!" said Snubby, triumphantly slapping his swimming trunks where he had hidden it. "What do you think of that?"

Everyone stared at Snubby, and nobody really knew what to think. Snubby always did such surprising things!

"Let's go back home and examine the letter," said Barney. "I don't know whether we ought to or not – but it does seem as if something peculiar must be going on. Why should Morgan, whoever he is, send a letter in code to a man like the one who knocked

you about so roughly? Why *in code*? If Morgan is only a fisherman, presumably he didn't write it – so someone else must have given it to him to hand to someone else – it was too secret and precious to be trusted to the post!"

"Do let's go and examine it," said Diana. "We might have to take it to the police, you know. But what could be going on in a little place like this – full of country folk and fishermen?"

"Smuggling, maybe?" suggested Roger, hopefully.

"What kind of smuggling could go on here?" said Barney. "No, I don't think it's that. In fact I can't imagine what it is. Come on – let's get back. Anyway, it's getting on for lunch-time."

Snubby smacked his lips at once. "Ha – good cooking – very good cooking!" he said. "Oh, by the way, I learned something from old Mrs Jones at the ice cream shop this morning, when I went to buy these super clothes. She told me that Mr Jones, who keeps our inn, is her son – and she said it's always been his dearest wish to own it, and now he does, because some rich friends he met when he was learning to be a chef in London, lent him the money to buy it."

"And I suppose those rich friends are Sir Somebody This and Sir Somebody That, whom she told us so often came down to stay," said Roger. "I bet they don't have to pay a penny when they come."

They were nearly at the inn now, and Barney gave Snubby a nudge. "We'll go to the caravan and see your letter there," he said. "We've plenty of time."

Soon all four, with Loony and Miranda, were shut in the caravan. Snubby was just about to show them the letter when Loony barked sharply.

"I bet that's Dafydd again, with that Waddle of a goose," said Diana, crossly, and opened the door. Yes, it was! He was up on the wheel, peering in at the window.

"Go away, you little snooper," said Diana, half amused, half cross.

"Soon be lunch," said Dafydd solemnly, his arm round the goose's neck.

"Well, we'll be in good time," said Diana. "Run away, now!"

She shut the door and they peered at the envelope Snubby took from his swimming trunks. "It's a bit squashed, because I've sat on it," he said, and slit the envelope. He drew out a one page sheet of paper, folded in four, and opened it out flat.

"There! It's in code, as we thought!" said Barney, excited. "We'll never decipher it, of course. Look at all the little figures and letters!"

"No wonder he thought that Bruce's letter

which I was trying to read was this one," said Snubby staring at it. "All this mess-up of figures and letters! Gosh – I wish we could decipher them."

"Well, we can't," said Barney, folding up the sheet. "What are we going to do with it? Shall we just wait and see if anything happens? The man who took your letter, Snubby, will soon find out that it's not the right one, because he won't be able to decode it – and if he could, he'd only read a lot of rubbish!"

"Well, I like that!" said Snubby indignantly. "Bruce and I don't write rubbish, let me tell you."

Nobody took any notice of his indignant remark. Diana spoke to Barney:

"And when the bearded man finds out that he's got the wrong letter – from a boy who wasn't the messenger after all – and that therefore someone else took the right letter from the fisher-boy and went off with it, what will he do?"

"Ah – what will he do?" said Barney, tickling Miranda under her chin. "I think we'd better wait and see – and in the meantime, we'll keep this letter very carefully!"

13

Two More Visitors at the Inn

Miss Pepper came to the caravan, just as the four children were getting up to go. She looked sharply at Snubby, fearing that he might be wearing his dreadful clothes – but he was still in his swimming trunks. The old clothes were on one of the bunks.

"You can throw those away, Snubby," she said. "See, here are your own things, washed and ironed. Please put them on."

"Can't I come in to lunch like this?" said Snubby, looking down at himself.

"No," Miss Pepper said definitely. "Diana, how brown you are getting! Did you have a nice morning?"

They went off together talking. Barney had been thinking deeply, and now he turned to Snubby and Roger. "I think it wouldn't be a bad idea to walk over to the fishing jetty this afternoon and see if we can spot this Morgan, and perhaps talk to him if we can," he said. "I'd like to see what kind of a fellow he is – and wouldn't I like to know what he's mixed up in!"

"Good idea!" said Snubby at once. "Do you hear that, Loony. Walkie-walk for you this afternoon!"

Loony promptly went mad and raced round the little caravan at top speed, jumping from bunk to bunk, barking.

"Er – Loony," said Barney, "sorry to disappoint you, old fellow – but you're not coming with us this afternoon!"

"Why ever not?" demanded Snubby, astonished.

"Use your brains!" said Barney. "If that boy who gave you the letter is there, he'd recognise Loony at once and even though you wouldn't be in swimming things this time, he'd perhaps recognise you if you had Loony with you. But without Loony, and wearing ordinary clothes, I don't see how he *could* recognise you."

"Loony won't like not coming," Snubby said, gloomily. "And he'll bark the place down if we leave him in the caravan."

"Well – we'll get Di to stay with Miss Pepper this afternoon and keep Loony with her," said Barney. "It's either that, or we leave you behind with Loony, Snubby."

"Oh, Diana will have Loony all right," said Snubby. "Stop showing off, Loony please – we all know about your wonderful jumping. Look what you've done to my bedclothes, you ass!"

They went off to the dining-room of the inn and found Diana at the table and Miss Pepper at the sideboard, putting slices of cold ham on to plates. Snubby went to help her, and Loony at once sat himself exactly below Miss Pepper's right arm, hoping she might perhaps drop a slice of ham!

Barney told Diana in a low voice what he proposed to do that afternoon, and she was quite willing to stay behind with Miss Pepper and Loony. "We could all three go for a little walk," she said. "Miss Pepper would like that. By the way – there are two more visitors at the inn!"

"Who?" asked Barney, looking round the table, pleased to see an enormous salad and mounds of new potatoes. "My word – what a fine spread!"

"I don't know their names," said Diana, "but look – here they come now!"

Two men walked into the room, one tall and commanding, with wire-framed spectacles and a smart, upturned moustache. The other was a short man with a black beard and sunglasses.

Snubby turned at that moment to take two plates of ham to the table and at once saw the two men. He jumped violently and a piece of ham leaped off one plate, and was at once snapped up by a delighted Loony. Snubby went quickly to the table and hissed at the surprised Barney and

Roger, nudging them and nodding over towards the table by the window where the two men sat with their backs to them.

The boys knew immediately what he meant! The man with the beard and the sunglasses was the one who had snatched Snubby's letter from him! Good gracious – and he was staying at the hotel!

"Has he seen Loony, do you think?" whispered Snubby. "He might recognise him. He can't recognise me, I'm sure, now I'm properly dressed."

"Take Loony out at once," ordered Barney. "Quick – before they see him. Here, stick a piece of my ham into his mouth, then he won't mind what you do with him! Lock him into the caravan."

Snubby snatched a piece of ham from one of the plates, picked up Loony, and put it into his mouth. Loony was so amazed at this extraordinary generosity that he didn't even bark. Snubby was able to streak out of the room with him at top speed, certain that the men hadn't seen him.

Miss Pepper was astonished to see him carrying Loony out of the room. "Was he sick or something?" she asked, sitting down at the table. "Poor Loony! Perhaps he swallowed too much seawater this morning."

"You never know," said Barney, and changed the subject at once. "This must be home-cured ham, mustn't it, Miss Pepper? It's got a wonderful flavour!"

"It probably is," said Miss Pepper. "Diana, pass me the salad cream, please."

Snubby came back, grinning. "I'm sorry that Loony felt sick," said Miss Pepper.

"He'd better stay behind this afternoon," Barney said solemnly, "and perhaps go for a walk with you, Miss Pepper – and Diana, too?"

"Yes. That's a good idea," said Diana. "Would you like me to go for a walk with you, Miss Pepper?"

Miss Pepper was really delighted. "We'll go up into the hills," she said. "And you could take your binoculars with you, Diana, and your bird book, and we could try to spot some interesting birds for your school essay."

Roger winked at Barney. Everything was going along very nicely!

Snubby kept staring at the two men and Barney kicked him to make him stop. Who were these men? It should be easy to find out from Mrs Jones. He grinned secretly to himself to think that one of them probably had Snubby's secret-code letter from his friend Bruce in his pocket – and had probably tried a dozen times to decode it, and failed!

Barney had a chance of finding out who the men were immediately after the meal. The two of them walked out of the room and went upstairs and Mrs Jones came in to clear away, with Dafydd and Waddle hovering about outside in the hall as usual.

"Two more visitors, I see, Mrs Jones," said Barney as she stopped to stroke Miranda, and give her a titbit.

"Oh, yes – they come often," said Mrs Jones proudly. "They are Sir Richard Ballinor and Professor Hallinan – he's the great bird expert, you know. They are friends of my husband, he met them in London, and they know his cooking is good, very good, so they come here often, and they love the place, they love the mountains and the hills and the sea, and . . ."

The boys waited patiently till she had run on for some time, then Barney interrupted.

"I expect they were pleased when your husband bought this place," he said. "It makes a nice holiday spot for them, doesn't it?"

"Ah, the good kind men, they lent my husband the money to buy the inn he so much wanted," said Mrs Jones, in her lilting Welsh voice. "So always I welcome them and give them my very best."

"I expect they've got that best room of yours then!" said Diana at once. Mrs Jones nodded.

"But that is not the room they like best," she said. "The room they always have is the room you have, with the two windows. But there – that Miss Pepper of yours is not one to change her mind, is she?"

"No, she's not," said Roger and Diana together, remembering how many times in the past they had tried to make Miss Pepper change her mind about something! And then they heard Miss Pepper's voice at the door.

"Aren't you coming, children? Loony is barking his head off in the caravan!"

"Right," said Barney, and they left Mrs Jones, who would certainly have chattered on for an hour if they had stayed!

Miss Pepper and Diana and Loony set off for their walk in the hills, Diana with the binoculars slung over her back. Loony was rather puzzled that Snubby didn't come with them and was inclined to stay with him, but when Snubby artfully rolled into his bunk and pretended to go to sleep, Loony at once decided that a walk with Diana was better than an afternoon in a boring caravan, with everyone shushing him.

"Now let's take our swimming things and go all the way along the beach to the fishing jetty," said Roger. "We can swim whenever we like – either before we look for Morgan, or afterwards."

"Better be afterwards," said Barney. "It's idiotic to swim too soon after lunch."

They set off with Miranda scampering in front of them, only leaping on to Barney's shoulder when they met a dog or a shouting child. The sun shone out of a cloudless sky and became very hot indeed as they walked over the white sand, past the caves.

They came near the little stone fishing jetty. Not many people were there. A few old boatmen sat on the low sun-warmed wall, and a woman sat knitting on a wooden seat. Barney and the others lay down on the sand nearby.

A dirty, unkempt boy in a bright woollen jersey came running on to the jetty with a crossbred poodle, and Barney sat up at once, nudging the others. "That's the boy who gave Snubby the letter," he said. "There can only be one poodle like that in this little place, surely!"

They all sat up and watched the boy. He went to where a boat was being untied and helped to push it off. It was a pretty sight to see its sails unfurling and filling with wind.

A man came on to the jetty at that moment, dressed in fisherman's clothes – a man who limped badly and walked with a stick. He went to talk to some old cronies on the wall. "Come on – let's go up on the jetty. We might be able to find out who Morgan is," said Roger.

But before they had got up from the sands someone else strode on to the jetty – a man with a dark beard, wearing sunglasses. He called sharply to the fisherman, who got up at once. "Here, Morgan – I want a word with you!"

"I bet there's going to be a quarrel!" said Barney excitedly. "Let's hope we hear it. Come on – we'll get nearer to the wall!"

14

An Exciting Afternoon

"Come over here," said Morgan to the bearded man, and took him to one side of the jetty, out of hearing of the other fishermen there. Barney and the others crawled over the sand as near as they dared, and lay down hidden by the stone jetty wall.

"Morgan – that letter you gave your nephew to deliver to me," began the man. "That wasn't the one you were given for me, you know it wasn't."

"What are you talking about, Sir Richard," said Morgan in a deep, puzzled voice. "That letter never left my pocket, and that I swear, from the time it came to me till the time I gave it to Dai this morning. Didn't he go to the pile of rocks we arranged?"

"Yes. He was there – dressed as you said, and the little black dog too, so I knew it was the right boy," said the bearded man. "But I tell you he gave me the wrong letter. I can't make head or tail of any of it!"

"That was the letter given to me for you," said Morgan obstinately. "Jim gave it to me as usual, straight from his pocket to mine it went, and all he said was, 'We'll be back Friday. Be ready,' and off he sailed again. That letter was what he gave me, I tell you."

"I don't understand it," said the bearded man, staring at Morgan. "Where's that nephew of yours? I'll have to question him – though how he could have changed the letter beats me. Morgan, if you're double-crossing me I'll pay you out in a way you won't like!"

"I'm not double-crossing anyone!" said Morgan, raising his voice angrily. "Do I want to double-cross myself? I'm in this as much as you are, aren't I?"

"Don't shout like that," said the other man, looking round anxiously, afraid of the other fishermen hearing.

"I'll call Dai," Morgan said surlily. "He's there, watching that boat. He'll tell you it was the letter all right. Dai! Dai! Here a minute!"

The small boy and the poodle came running up. "Yes, Uncle Morgan?" said Dai, glancing at the bearded man, and looking scared.

"Did you give this gentleman the letter I gave you for him this morning?" his uncle asked sternly.

"Yes," lied the boy. "Yes, of course I did."

The bearded man suddenly caught hold of the small boy and held him in such a fierce grip that he began to howl. "You didn't give me any letter! You're not the boy I saw! He was bigger – and his dog was a black spaniel, not a poodle."

"Let go of the boy," said Morgan sternly, seeing that Dai was scared almost to death. "You said you had a letter given to you by a boy – who was the boy then, if it wasn't Dai?"

"I don't know. I tell you, it was a boy with a spaniel – a real ragamuffin, like your nephew," said the man, glaring at the terrified boy. "And when I came up to him, I saw he was actually reading the letter! It was in code. I immediately thought that it was the letter he should have delivered to me and took it, though he tried to stop me."

Morgan laughed harshly, and turned away. "Then you are a fool, Sir Richard. The boy wasn't the right ragamuffin, and the letter was his, not yours."

Sir Richard grasped Morgan's arm and swung him round. "Man, this is urgent, you know that. I've not got the right letter, I tell you – the letter you gave to Dai. Where's *that* letter? You, boy, answer me at once!"

"I – I gave it to a boy who came to talk

to me," wept poor Dai, terrified out of his life. "I waited and waited for you, and this boy said he'd give it to you for me. I didn't know you'd already been and gone off with the wrong letter."

Sir Richard pushed the boy away from him with such force that he almost toppled over into the water. Morgan scowled. "Leave the boy alone. What harm's been done? You got a letter you couldn't read and someone else has got a letter he can't read. I'll get in touch with Jim and he'll send another."

Sir Richard took out a handkerchief and mopped his forehead. He came close to Morgan and spoke in his ear, so that the three boys listening down on the sand below the jetty could only just hear his words.

"You deliver the next letter to me yourself, Morgan. If anything goes wrong, it'll be laid on your shoulders for thinking that idiotic nephew of yours was trustworthy. If Jim's letter hadn't been in code, there'd be someone else now who would know enough to spoil all our plans for Friday – yes, and for always!"

"Aw, shut up," said Morgan rudely, and turned away.

"And if I find that boy whose letter I took – and who took my letter from Dai – I'll wring his neck!" said Sir Richard in such a bloodthirsty tone that Snubby, who could hear every word, felt suddenly scared. What had seemed rather a peculiar joke was turning into something that wasn't a joke at all! Why on earth had he gone and talked to Dai and persuaded him to hand over the letter?

"I'd know the boy anywhere," went on Sir Richard, still in the same angry voice. "Awful ragamuffin – a tramp of a lad in dirty-looking trousers, a horrible jersey and a peaked cap too big for him – and a black spaniel. Dai is dressed much the same, but he isn't as big as this other fellow, and the black dog misled me, of course."

Snubby was feeling distinctly uncomfortable now, and so were Barney and Roger. How maddening that this fellow was staying at the inn! Would he recognise Loony? And then Snubby?

Morgan strode off, leaving the other man by himself. The fishermen on the wall looked at Morgan curiously as he passed. They had been too far away to hear anything that was said but they knew there had been a quarrel.

"Your grand friend upset, Morgan?" called one old fellow. "Wasn't your last catch of fish good enough for his lordship?"

Morgan didn't answer. The fishermen nudged one another and grinned as the bearded man walked after Morgan, but nobody dared call out to him. Dai had disappeared entirely, hidden somewhere out of sight.

The three boys on the sand lay there silently for some time and then, hearing no more voices, rolled over and looked at one another. "Let's go and swim," said Barney, in case anyone was listening. He added in a low voice, "We'll talk later. Come on."

"Yes – a swim would be good, it's so hot," said Roger loudly. Snubby said nothing. He was still very shaken by what he had overheard. He hoped the letter was safe in the caravan. Had he better destroy it?

They said no more till they were well away from the jetty. Barney mopped his head and said, "Whew! What on earth do we do next? You've landed us into something now, Snubby – all through that idiotic code letter from Bruce."

"It wasn't idiotic," said Snubby in a rather meeker voice than usual. "Anyway, that fellow – fancy him being the Sir Richard Mrs Jones told us about – couldn't puzzle out our code. It's a jolly good one and not idiotic as you seem to think."

"Let's swim," said Barney, "and perhaps when we feel a bit cooler we can think this business out. Good thing we didn't bring Loony, Snubby, that fellow might have spotted him – and us."

"I say, what on earth are we going to do with Loony now?" said Snubby in sudden dismay. "We mustn't let that fellow, Sir Richard, see him at all, but you know what Loony is – rushing about all over the place!"

They all splashed into the cool sea, and when they came out they felt decidedly better. They sat on the sand and talked.

"Today's Wednesday – and whatever is going to happen is planned for Friday. I think it's smuggling," said Roger. "There are only two more days to go. Do we go to the police, do you think?"

"No. No, I don't think so. If we do, they will question that bearded fellow, and whatever's planned won't happen," said Barney, frowning. "I'm just thinking of something we heard one of the fishermen yell out to Morgan. He said 'Wasn't your last catch of fish good enough for his lordship?' Well now, what did that mean? It means that Morgan hires out a boat to Sir Richard, presumably for catching fish – but perhaps brings in something else – either instead of fish, or hidden in the catch."

"Something that he wants brought here to be hidden, do you think?" asked Roger.

"Yes. Perhaps something he wants to hide for some considerable time," Barney said thoughtfully. "I wonder who this Sir Richard really is, and his friend Professor Hallinan, the bird expert. I think they are just posing as Sir Richard and the Professor – using their names instead of their own. I think I'll walk into Dilcarmock and telephone my father after tea, and ask him if he can find out."

"They must be rich, to lend Mr Jones the money to buy the inn," said Snubby, screwing his toes into the sand.

"I can't think why anyone should lend so much money to a fellow like Mr Jones, just because they liked his cooking so much," said Barney. "I mean, when you lend money, you expect to get some good return from it – the profits made on the visitors that come to the inn, for instance. But very little profit can be made on that inn, I'm sure. Beside ourselves there are only those two men there!"

"Well, what does he give them in return then?" said Snubby. "Do you imagine he lets them use his inn as a kind of headquarters for whatever they are really up to?"

Barney sat up straight and smacked his knee. "Of course! You've hit it! What other reason could there be? There's a little gang here, Morgan and Jim – whoever he is – and Mr Jones, all in some game together, and this inn is somehow the heart of it. Gosh – we *have* tumbled on to something!"

"But *what* have we tumbled on?" asked Snubby, excited. "How can we find out what it is? I say – this is pretty exciting, isn't it? I simply can't wait till Friday!"

15

Oh, Loony!

Loony was extremely glad to see the boys when they came back, and rather astonished to be shut up immediately in the caravan, when everyone went to have tea. He barked dismally and Miss Pepper was surprised at Snubby's seeming hard-heartedness.

"I really can't see why he can't come in to tea," she said. "He was as good as gold with us this afternoon. We had a wonderful walk and Diana spotted some most unusual birds with the binoculars."

"There was one bird I couldn't make out," said Diana. "A green bird with a red topknot."

"Mrs Jones tells me that there is a Professor Hallinan staying here," said Miss Pepper. "A famous ornithologist, and—"

"A what?" said Snubby, astonished.

"Bird expert," said Miss Pepper. "So I suggested that Diana should ask him about the bird. He'd be sure to be able to identify it."

The three boys felt extremely doubtful about this, as none of them believed that the Professor was a real birdman, any more than Sir Richard was really a Sir Anybody! But Barney winked at the boys, and said cheerfully, "Yes, Di, good idea. I'll come with you and listen to what he says. Might learn something – you never know!"

Snubby gave a sudden chuckle. "No, you never know!" he said. "Miss Pepper, we're going to walk into Dilcarmock after tea – coming?"

"Good gracious no! I've had enough walking today," said Miss Pepper. "You'd better catch a bus part of the way, it's quite a distance."

The two men came in to tea at that moment and nodded to Miss Pepper. Diana decided to catch Professor Hallinan when he went out of the room. So she hovered about with Barney, while Snubby and Roger went to comfort poor Loony in the caravan.

At last the men came walking out and made for the stairs. Diana darted to the tall moustached one, with glasses.

"Oh, please do excuse me, Professor Hallinan," she said breathlessly. "But I know you are a famous ornith – ornith – whatever it is, and know all about birds, so do you think you could help me to name a bird I saw today?"

"Er – surely! I'd be pleased to try," said

the Professor. "Where did you see it?"

"Flying over the hills," said Diana. "Green, with a red topknot."

"Ah well, I fear I couldn't identify a bird on so little description," said the Professor, courteously. "It sounds as if it might be a rare immigrant which is sometimes seen here – Latin name *Lateus hillemus*. Yes, it might be that."

"Oh thank you," said Diana. "I hope I shall remember such a peculiar name!"

Barney now entered the conversation, very politely. "I saw a short-necked curlikew," he said, "just outside the inn, it was. Surely that was unusual?"

"Very unusual," said the Professor.

"And would you say that dotty shade warblers could be found in these hills?" asked Barney. "I have heard they nest at times."

"Er – well, yes, I believe they have been known to nest here," said the Professor. "Excuse me – I must join my friend." And away he went up the stairs.

Diana stared at Barney in the utmost amazement. "Short-necked curlikews! I've never heard of them in my life," she said, "and I know the names of most of our birds now. And whoever heard of dotty shade warblers?"

"Nobody," said Barney, taking her arm. "Your professor is a fraud, Diana. What did he say that green bird of yours was – a *Lateus hillimus*? Poppycock! You won't find that bird in any of your bird books! He's no more a bird expert than I am. I only wish I'd asked him if he had ever seen the curious nest of a poppy cockbird."

Diana giggled. "Gracious! I've a good mind to put the poppy cockbird into my school essay, just for a joke – and draw one too. But I say, Barney, do you really think the Professor is a fraud? He was so polite, and knowledgeable too."

"All tricksters are," said Barney. "And I bet that his friend, Sir Richard as he calls himself, is no more a botanist than the Professor is a bird expert! They're frauds, both of them – pretending to be what they're not. My father knew their names but I bet if he met them here, he would have spotted that they were bogus. Anyway, I'm going to phone him and ask him to make some inquiries, so that we can be certain."

"Well, let's go and break the news to the others," said Diana. "Come on. Goodness – to think that the bogus Professor said that your equally bogus dotty shade warblers could be found in these hills! How do you think of names like that, Barney?"

"It's easy!" said Barney. "Come on, Di. I want to be off to Dilcarmock to telephone my father. And we must keep Loony out of Sir Richard's sight, there's no doubt about that. He'd recognise him at once!"

They went halfway to Dilcarmock by bus, and then walked the rest of the way. Loony was delighted. Two long walks in a day – he was truly in luck!

Barney telephoned his father. "Dad? It's Barney here. Can you hear me?"

"Yes – speak up a little though," said his father. "Are you all right?"

"Fine," said Barney. "But there's a bit of a mystery about two men here – the famous experts that old Mrs Jones at the ice cream shop told us about . . . Sir Richard Ballinor and Professor Hallinan – they've arrived at the inn and I've a feeling they're frauds – no more experts than I am! The Professor doesn't know one bird from another. What are they like, Dad? The real men, I mean?"

"One is tall, with an upturned moustache and wears glasses," said his father. "And the other, Sir Richard, is rather short, and has a beard."

"Gosh," said Barney, surprised to hear his father give such a close description of the two men at the inn. "That pretty well describes the two fellows here, Dad, the ones I think are frauds. I say – could you possibly find out if the real Sir Richard and the real Professor are at their homes? If they are, I'll know for certain these two fellows are frauds, and we'll watch them to see what they are up to. But if you hear they're away in Wales – well – I suppose they won't be frauds after all. I think they are, though, in fact I'm sure of it!"

His father chuckled. "Quite a mystery!" he said. "I'll certainly find out where the real Sir Richard and Professor are – they're both members of my club and I can easily inquire there. I'll let you know as soon as possible whether your two men are false or genuine."

"Thanks, Dad," said Barney.

"Right. But don't get mixed up in anything unpleasant, Barney," said his father. "Let me know if there's anything I can do to help. I'll find out what you want at once, and you'll know tonight. Now don't get into any trouble – if these men aren't what they seem, they may be most unpleasant if they think any snooping is going on."

"Right, Dad. Thanks again and goodbye," said Barney and put down the receiver. He went out of the box and told the others what his father had said. "We'll know for certain tonight if what we think is correct," he said. "I bet we're on the right track!"

The four walked halfway back and caught the bus the rest of the way, feeling quite tired. Even Loony decided that it was possible to overdo this walking habit!

Miranda, of course, loved it all, for she sat on Barney's shoulder most of the time and was thoroughly spoilt by all the passengers in the bus! "You'll be sick down my neck if you accept any more sweets from people," said Barney at last. "Stop nibbling my ear, Miranda, you tickle!"

At a few minutes before eight that evening the telephone rang, and Mrs Jones came hurrying into the room where everyone was sitting to get Barney, who shot out to the phone.

"Well, we guessed right," said Barney, coming back into the room. "Mr Jones's rich and important friends are no more than rogues who are making money in some dishonest way with his help! Rogues who are working in disguise and using other men's names! Now we can go right ahead and try and find out what's happening. Friday night is apparently the night. If only we knew what we were looking for!" Diana wanted to tell Miss Pepper, but nobody agreed.

"But all this sounds as if it might be dangerous," said Diana. "And surely the police ought to be told those men are frauds."

"We'll wait till Friday comes and see if we can find out what is happening," said Barney. "And for goodness sake, let's keep Loony out of sight. If one of those men spots him and guesses that he belongs to one of us, there will be danger because they'll know Loony's owner has got the real letter, and they'll go for Snubby at once to get their precious letter!"

"All right. Let's destroy it then!" Snubby said promptly.

"No," said Barney. "We might have to produce it, to show we really did get hold of it – when the police come in on the job as they'll have to sooner or later. I'll take it and hide it somewhere safe. I'll get it now."

He went out of the room and down to the caravan. The letter had been put into Snubby's pillowcase, on his bunk. Barney slipped in his hand and took it out. Then he found some sticky-tape and took it and the code letter outside the caravan. He crawled underneath it and taped the letter on the under-part of the caravan, very firmly indeed. He crept out, grinning. If anyone

found it there he would be very very clever!

Loony was sitting sadly by himself in the caravan, wondering why he wasn't allowed in the inn. Barney felt sorry for him and left Miranda there for company. The little monkey sat close to Loony, chattering in his ear, but he took no notice at all. He was waiting for his beloved Snubby to come for him!

Everyone went to bed early that night, for they were very tired.

"What with swimming and walking, and all the rest of the excitement we've had, I can't keep awake another minute!" said Snubby, with a tremendous yawn that set all the others off too, Miss Pepper as well.

"Come along, Diana," she said, getting up. "You go off to your caravan, boys. Sleep well!"

They all slept very well indeed, and Diana didn't want to get up when the tea arrived next morning, brought as usual by Mrs Jones, followed by Daffyd and the goose!

"Oh, Mrs Jones – I don't think we need have the goose in here," protested Miss Pepper, and Mrs Jones shooed both the little boy and Waddle away.

"I didn't even know they were behind me," she said. "That Dafydd, he puts his nose in everywhere, and that goose, he is just as bad – in my larder he was yesterday, Miss Pepper, as sure as I stand here, pecking at the scones I had made for tea. Sir

Richard and the Professor, they make such a fuss of my Dafydd, Miss Pepper, he follows them all day long, they spoil him, I say, and—"

"Well, thank you, Mrs Jones, we'll be down in half an hour," said Miss Pepper firmly, knowing quite well that if she didn't interrupt Mrs Jones, she would be standing there talking till breakfast time!

Everyone was punctual for breakfast for once, and Sir Richard and the Professor were at their table too. Nobody knew Dafydd and the goose were once more peeping in at the window of the caravan – and that Dafydd was feeling very sorry for Loony, left there to wait for Snubby to return.

"Poor dog Loony," said Dafydd softly, and tapped on the window. "Poor dog!"

Loony saw Dafydd's small face peering in at the window and barked hopefully, pawing at the window pane as he stood on his hind paws on one of the bunks.

"Dafydd will undo the door for poor dog Loony," said the small boy pityingly. "Wait, dog Loony." He scrambled down from the wheel he was standing on and, with his goose behind him, went to the door. It was shut, not locked, and he opened it easily.

Loony shot out at top speed, barking, and the goose fled for its life, cackling as if it had laid a hundred eggs. Dafydd was cross.

He had at least expected a word of thanks from Loony!

Loony tore across the slope of the hill and into the hall of the inn, the door of which was always left open. Where was Snubby? He flung himself against the door of the dining-room and scampered in, barking delightedly.

"Loony!" said Snubby in horror. "You bad dog! How did you get out?"

Loony threw himself on Snubby and licked him, whimpering as if he hadn't seen Snubby for a month. Barney glanced quickly round at the two men at the window table, with their bacon and eggs in front of them. Sir Richard was staring at Loony in amazement, and he nudged the Professor. "That's the dog!" he said. "I'd know him anywhere. He belongs to that boy, see?"

Barney couldn't hear what was said, but he could guess. Now the men would know that Snubby was the boy who had their letter. "Quick, Snubby!" he said. "Let's get out of here with Loony. Hurry up! Those men have spotted him – and you too!"

16

A Day Out For Snubby!

Snubby was really scared. He got up at once and, followed by Barney, left the table and went quickly out of the door. Loony went too, barking in delight. Miss Pepper was astonished by their behaviour, and stared after them indignantly.

"Where have they gone – and why did they leave the breakfast table without a word to me?" she said. "Is one of them feeling ill, Diana?"

Roger gave Diana a little kick under the table, afraid she might say something that would make trouble. "Er – didn't you think Snubby looked a little pale?" he said. "Perhaps it's a touch of the sun. He may have said a word to Barney about it."

"I'd better go and find out," said Miss Pepper.

"Oh, wait till Barney comes back," said Roger. "Don't leave your hot bacon and eggs! I expect old Barney will be back in a minute."

He shot a glance at the two men sitting at the window table. They were talking earnestly, and the bearded man looked angry and troubled. Roger wished he could hear what they were saying.

Snubby was now safely in the caravan with Barney, Loony at his feet, and Miranda cuddled in Barney's arms. They were talking earnestly.

"How did Loony get out? He can't open the door himself!" said Snubby. "I bet it was that little nuisance of a Dafydd – always snooping round! Well the fat's in the fire now! Those men spotted Loony all right – and know I'm the boy who took the code letter from that fraud Sir Richard."

"Yes, and they're certain to try and get it now," said Barney. "How, I don't know – but it might be rather unpleasant for you, Snubby, if they catch you! I think the best thing for you to do is to hide."

"All right. But where?" asked Snubby dismally. "In the caravan? They'd soon find me here."

"No, certainly not in the caravan," said Barney. "I almost think the best thing to do would be to catch the next bus into Dilcarmock and spend the day there. Unless the men happened to see you getting on the bus they'd never guess you'd gone there. I'd better come with you."

"Yes, do," said Snubby, still looking

dismal. "But what on earth are we going to tell Miss Pepper?"

"The truth!" said Barney, getting up. "I'll see if I can catch Roger's ear and tell him what we're going to do, and he can tell Miss Pepper we decided to go to Dilcarmock and rushed out to catch the bus – and apologise for us."

"I never finished my bacon and eggs," groaned Snubby. "Oh, why did I ever get mixed up with that idiotic letter?"

"I'll see if I can catch Roger," said Barney, and ran up to the inn. He was careful not to be seen from the dining-room window, for he knew the men sat there. He went to the dining-room door and peeped in. Miss Pepper had her back to him, and he was able to signal to Roger unseen.

"Excuse me a moment, Miss Pepper," said Roger, and slipped out of the room before she could ask him any questions. She was puzzled and annoyed.

"What is everyone doing this morning?" she said. "I hope you feel all right, Diana. I really think I'd better go and see what is happening."

"Well, have some hot toast first," said Diana, trying to give the boys as much time as she could. "Take this nice brown piece."

Barney told Roger their plans in a few words. "We think Snubby had better clear off for the day so we're going in to

Dilcarmock by bus and won't be back till suppertime. Then I'll lock Snubby into the caravan, and we'll say he's tired, and I'll take him something to eat there – and perhaps have it with him, in case those men try to get him. Got it?"

"Yes," said Roger. "But Miss Pepper is getting very suspicious. For goodness sake go now – she'll be out in half a minute, I know she will."

"Right. We'll go at once," said Barney, and went to fetch Snubby from the caravan. Roger watched them go racing down the slope to the village below. Would they catch the bus? It was about due now, and if they missed it they would have to wait a whole hour. He went back to the inn and met Miss Pepper hurrying out, having eaten her bacon, eggs and toast very quickly.

"Oh, Roger! What is happening?" she asked. "Really! Leaving the table like that, one after the other, without a word of explanation! Where are Snubby and Barney?"

Roger looked round carefully before he answered, in case the man might be within hearing. "Well, it's all quite simple," he said, smiling brightly. "Apparently they made up their minds to go to Dilcarmock for the day, and had to rush off very suddenly to catch the bus. They asked me to apologise to you."

"Well – why in the world couldn't they have said just one word to me about their plans," said Miss Pepper, still puzzled. "Aren't you and Diana going?"

"Er – no – we thought we'd stay here and keep you company," said Roger. "What about going out in a boat, Miss Pepper, just us three?"

"Well, that would be very nice," said Miss Pepper. "Very nice indeed. But I shall have a few words to say to Barney and Snubby when they come back this evening – tearing out of the room like that in the middle of breakfast!"

The two men came out of the inn at that moment, talking in low tones, looking all round. Roger was sure they were looking for Snubby. They looked at him, and Sir Richard took a step forward as if he were going to say something. Then the other man pulled him by the arm, to stop him. Obviously nothing was going to be said in front of Miss Pepper!

"I bet they know she'd call the police if they began to make a rumpus about Snubby and secret letters!" thought Roger. He was glad to see Diana coming out of the inn behind the men.

"Di! We're going boating!" he shouted. "Just the right morning for it – hot sun and a wind off the shore."

"Oh good!" said Diana, longing to know

what had happened to Snubby and Barney, but not daring to ask in front of Miss Pepper. Roger took Diana's arm and hurried her off to the caravan. "Just going to tidy up the bunks!" he called. "We'll be ready in ten minutes' time."

Diana thought it was a very good idea of Barney's to go to Dilcarmock for the day. "If only we can get Friday over, with whatever's supposed to happen then, I'll feel safer!" she said. "Oh dear – why does Snubby always get into trouble? And us with him! And he never seems to mind, does he? I bet he's sitting happily in the bus now, pretending to play a banjo or something, and keeping everyone in fits of laughter."

Diana was almost right in her guess! Snubby *was* in the bus but he wasn't playing a pretend banjo, he was playing a mouth-organ – or rather, pretending to, his hand up to his mouth, making a most realistic *zz-zz-zz* noise, exactly as if he was playing a jiggy tune. And as Diana had surmised, everyone was delighted, laughing and egging him on. No, Snubby wasn't feeling nearly as worried as the others!

When Miranda slid down to the floor and began to dance in time to Snubby's horrible noises, even the bus driver had to look round and the bus almost went into a ditch!

"Shut up now, Snubby," said Barney, alarmed. "You'll cause an accident."

Back at the inn the others were preparing for a morning's boating. Miss Pepper insisted on large sunhats being taken, for the sun would beat down on the boat and there would be no shelter at all. They all had to go and buy some at old Mrs Jones's shop, which meant an ice cream each, of course.

While they were eating them, the two men from the inn passed slowly by and peered in. They said nothing, much to Roger's relief, and walked on.

"I don't like those men," said Miss Pepper. "I can't imagine why they're down here – they don't seem to fish or swim – and look, they're in their city suits even on a day like this! If they weren't who they are I'd think they were up to no good!"

"I wouldn't be surprised if you're right, Miss Pepper," said Roger solemnly, and Diana gave a sudden giggle.

They had a glorious morning quite far out in a boat. They took turns at rowing and steering and lying flat with a hand over the side dragging through the water. The two children swam from the boat as well, and slowly their faces, arms and legs turned a bright red-brown. Miss Pepper was extremely glad of her enormous sunhat!

Barney and Snubby also had quite an amusing time in Dilcarmock. It was a big seaside town, full of trippers, and had a tremendous lot of sideshows. Barney, who

had once been a circus-boy, used to going round with fairs, enjoyed joining in the amusements he had known so well: hoop-la stalls, dodgem cars, swings, roundabouts and so on. He even met someone he had once known quite well, and they had a wonderful talk which poor Snubby couldn't even share.

Miranda loved it all, of course, and Loony met so many stray dogs tearing about that he had the time of his life. He thought Dilcarmock was much more interesting than Penrhyndendraith!

"Time to get the bus back," said Barney at last. "We shall miss supper at the inn if we don't – even though you must have had at least a dozen ice creams, Snubby, and goodness knows how many shrimps, and some of that awful gingerbread, and three meat-pies, and – let me see – how many cheese sandwiches was it?"

"Well, I'm beginning to feel hungry for my supper, all the same," said Snubby. "So don't let's miss the bus, Barney. Loony, keep to heel. I don't want to lose you just as the bus is due."

They went to the bus stop, and the bus came rumbling along in about two minutes. They settled into the front seats, Miranda on Barney's shoulder, eager to see everything as usual. Loony lay at Snubby's feet.

"I do hope those men won't try to get me this evening," said Snubby suddenly. "I'd forgotten all about them, I was enjoying myself so. Do you think I dare go in to supper?"

"Yes, you'll be all right if we're all with you," said Barney. "But we must go about together, all four of us and Loony, till bed-time. We can say we're jolly tired and go off early, see?"

They were glad to walk up the slope to the caravan, for they really were tired. Roger was there, waiting for them with an anxious face.

"I say!" he said, as soon as he saw them. "Something's happened – the code letter's gone from under the caravan where Barney stuck it. I think that silly, snooping little Dafydd found it. I can't find the little wretch anywhere, or I'd take it from him – and I only hope the men don't see him with it! Isn't he a pest?"

17

Where is the Code Letter?

Barney and Snubby looked at Roger in horror. The code letter had gone? Who would have thought that anyone could possibly find it, fixed so neatly to the underside of the caravan?

"Not only that – but our caravan lock was broken when I went down to it after tea and the whole place was upside down!"

"That must have been the two men searching it for the letter," said Barney at once. "Dafydd wouldn't dare to do that. He wouldn't be able to break the lock for one thing."

"Why do you think Dafydd has the letter?" asked Snubby.

"Well, I'll tell you," said Roger. "You see, Miss Pepper, Di and I came back for lunch, and when I went to get something out of the caravan I saw Waddle the goose standing by it. The lock definitely wasn't broken then. I was surprised to see Waddle there all by himself, because he's like a dog, always at Dafydd's heels . . ."

"Where was Dafydd then – under the caravan?" asked Barney.

"Yes! I looked all round for him, and couldn't see him and then the goose stuck its head under the caravan and cackled as if to say 'Buck up, Dafydd!' And I looked under and there was the little pest as quiet as a mouse!"

"Did you see if he had the letter?" asked Snubby.

"No. I didn't think about the letter then," said Roger. "I just shouted at Dafydd and told him to come out, and said he wasn't to go near the caravan. He's too light-fingered – takes anything he fancies, like a monkey. Oh, I'm sorry, Miranda, I forgot you were present!"

Miranda chattered as if she understood, and Roger went on with his tale. "Well, Dafydd shot off with Waddle and then I remembered the letter and crawled under the caravan to have a look. And the letter wasn't there but there were bits of sticky-tape left behind so somebody must have pulled it off to get the letter. And I'm dead certain it was Dafydd, because if it had been the two men they wouldn't have come in the afternoon and searched the caravan for it, would they?"

"Not if they had taken the letter in the morning," said Barney. "Well now, the thing is, has that little pest still got the letter? We'd best find out as soon as we can."

But Dafydd had gone to bed! "He is fast asleep," said Mrs Jones. "Such a boy he has been today, and that goose of his! Into my larder they were, and up the stairs, and into mischief everywhere, and—"

"Er – would he like this little clock we won at hoop-la in Dilcarmock?" said Barney, bringing a little clock out of his pocket.

"Indeed and he would, oh indeed to goodness!" said Mrs Jones. "But not tonight, he is asleep! Tomorrow I will give it to him myself."

"No, I'd like to give it to him," said Barney, as he put the clock firmly back into his pocket and went off before Mrs Jones could say any more.

"We'll make him give up the letter in return for the clock," said Barney. "The little wretch! He's everywhere! Fancy crawling under the caravan!"

"Well, kids do silly things like that when they're as small as he is," said Snubby. "I remember thinking it was great fun to crawl under my uncle's car when I was his age and let oil drip on me."

"You would!" said Diana. "Ugh! Thank goodness I didn't want to do things like that."

They had a very pleasant supper and,

much to their surprise, the two men were not there.

"Have they gone, Mrs Jones?" asked Barney, nodding his head towards the window-table. She shook her head.

"Oh no. They had an early meal and have gone to see some friends. Busy men they are, even when they are down in quiet Penrhyndendraith – rich men, important men, and proud I am to think they like our inn – but it's the cooking, and very good cooking! You too like my husband's cooking, I know! You—"

"Yes, yes, Mrs Jones," said Miss Pepper, and the cheery little woman took the hint and scuttled out of the room.

"She's absolutely non-stop!" said Snubby. "Honestly, I never know why you stop her, Miss Pepper. I could listen to her for ages."

"I dare say," said Miss Pepper. "But you and I have slightly different ideas, Snubby."

"Don't squash me like that," said Snubby crossly. "Anyone would think I was an orange."

Miss Pepper simply couldn't stop laughing, and the others chuckled. "You can't squash old Snubby," said Roger. "We've all tried but he's made of rubber. He bounces back up again immediately."

They all went off to bed early again, really tired with their long day. The three boys held a conference in their caravan.

"I'll nab Dafydd first thing tomorrow morning if I can, and get that letter from him," said Barney. "And Snubby must be very careful not to go near the two men, in case they think he's got it on him – they know it's not hidden in the caravan, because they've searched for it. What a mess they made, the wretches!"

"How am I to stay away from the men tomorrow?" demanded Snubby. "I can't keep going off to Dilcarmock."

"We'll think of something," said Barney. He yawned. "I'm going to sleep – and woe betide Dafydd tomorrow if he doesn't give me that letter!"

The next morning they looked for Dafydd and Waddle as soon as they got up, but they were nowhere to be seen. Barney and Roger went along to the kitchen, where Mr Jones was cooking breakfast that smelled too delicious for words.

"Er – good morning. Do you know where Dafydd is?" asked Barney politely.

Mr Jones turned, scowling, holding a frying-pan in his hand. "No, I do not. I will not have him here when I cook."

The boys went out of the kitchen hurriedly, feeling that Mr Jones did not want them there either when he "cooked".

"What a miserable chap," said Roger. "You'd think he'd be pretty cheerful, having this inn for his own."

They kept a sharp eye out for the two men, but did not see them. Barney went cautiously into the dining-room to see if they were there and found Mrs Jones clearing dirty plates away from the men's table.

"Oh – have they had breakfast already?" asked Barney.

"Yes – early they were today!" said Mrs Jones. "Sir Richard, he said they had much business to do today, and—"

"Oh, he did, did he?" said Barney. "I wonder what kind of business he does in a little place like this."

"Sir Richard owns two fishing vessels," said Mrs Jones, "and many other things. He . . ."

But just then Miss Pepper came in with Diana, and Mrs Jones hurried out of the kitchen to tell Mr Jones they were down.

The boys went hunting for Dafydd again after breakfast, keeping a sharp lookout for the two men, who, however, were not to be seen. It wasn't until nearly lunch-time that they found Dafydd, wandering along with Waddle as usual. He came up to them at once.

"Mum says there is a clock you have," he said. "A clock for me."

"Oh, she told you, did she?" said Barney, taking the little clock out of his pocket.

Dafydd gazed at the clock in delight, and rattled something off in Welsh. He reached out for it but Barney held it away.

"Dafydd," he said, "if I give you this you must give *me* something."

"My knife!" said Dafydd, and dug his hand into his pocket.

"No, Dafydd, I want that paper you found under our caravan," said Barney. "You were bad to take it. But if you give it to me now, you shall have the clock."

"Paper gone," said Dafydd solemnly.

"Gone? Where's it gone?" asked Roger.

"Men took it," said Dafydd, pointing in the direction of the inn.

"When?" said Barney sharply.

Dafydd did not seem to know. He suddenly began to cry. "They shout at Dafydd," he said. "Dafydd sit there, to make a boat with the paper," and he pointed to a little wooden seat in the inn garden. "And man come and say 'You give me that!' and he take it – like this." And Dafydd made a grab at the clock Barney was holding.

"Good gracious!" said Roger. "That's a blow, isn't it? Dafydd, when was this?"

"Man hit Waddle," said Dafydd, aiming a blow in the air. "Bad man. Steal from Dafydd. You give me clock now?"

"No. You haven't got the letter to give me," said Barney sternly. "You were a bad boy to take the paper away and make a boat."

"He probably didn't think it was ours,"

said Roger, as the little boy began to cry bitterly. "After all, you don't usually find a sheet of paper stuck under a caravan! He couldn't have guessed it was so important."

"I suppose he couldn't," said Barney, looking at the sobbing child. He suddenly put his arm round him. "Stop crying. We forgive you. See, here is the clock – it says tick-a-tock, tick-a-tock!"

Dafydd was overjoyed. He stopped crying at once and took the clock. He held it to Waddle's ear. "Listen!" he said. "Tick-a-tock, tick-a-tock."

The goose backed away, not at all sure about the clock.

"This is how you set the alarm going," said Barney, hoping the child would understand. "See – you move this little switch – and now listen!"

The alarm shrilled out and the goose raced off in fright, cackling loudly. Dafydd was entranced. He suddenly put his arms round Barney and gave him a great big hug.

"You nice boy," he said. "Dafydd get back paper for you. Yes, Dafydd give it to you."

"I wish you could, old chap," said Barney. "But it's too late now! Run along."

Dafydd went to find his goose, and the others looked at one another hopelessly.

"No good," said Barney. "Those two men have the letter and know all they want to, whatever it is – they know what 'Jim' had told them to do tonight, and everything. Well, it's about lunch-time. Where's Miss Pepper?"

"I'll go and get her. She's upstairs," said Snubby. "Come on, Loony, let's go and tell Miss Pepper she's very late!"

And away he went at top speed with Loony, racing up the stairs. But Miss Pepper was not in her room, and Snubby turned to go down again, Loony running in front of him.

He stopped dead as he saw Sir Richard coming along the landing, out of the best room. The man saw him and rushed at him, catching him by the collar.

"You! You pest! How dare you take that letter from that boy, Dai! How much do you know? You tell me, or I'll throw you down the stairs."

He swung Snubby over the stairway as if he really meant to keep his word. Snubby, half choked, was terrified out of his life.

He gasped out something, but the man could not understand, and shook him as if he were a rat. "Answer me! I'll get the truth out of you if I choke you!"

Loony heard the angry voice and came tearing up at top speed. The little spaniel gave an angry snarl and flung himself on the man, nipping him sharply in the calf of the leg. Sir Richard let Snubby go, and yelled

with pain, and the boy at once fled into
Miss Pepper's room and locked the door
behind him.

He listened, gasping and choking, and
heard the man rush down the stairs, pursued
by a very angry Loony. Now what was he
to do? He simply dare not slip out of Miss
Pepper's room – that man might get him
again!

18

Dafydd's Discovery

Roger, Barney and Diana waited patiently for Snubby and Loony to come down with Miss Pepper. In a short while Miss Pepper appeared from the garden of the inn, where she had been sitting, reading a paper.

"Oh, are you ready for lunch?" she asked. "Where's Snubby?"

The others looked at one another. Where was Snubby – and why hadn't he come down when he found that Miss Pepper wasn't in her room? Barney felt suddenly alarmed.

"I'll fetch him," he said, and went into the inn. He tore up the stairs, and came to Miss Pepper's room. It was shut and locked. Loony was there scratching at the door whining. Barney knocked. "Snubby! Are you there?"

Snubby's voice answered him, sounding rather weak. "Yes. Oh, Barney, is it you? I'll unlock the door."

He unlocked it and Barney went in at

once. "What have you done to your head?" he said. "My word, you look awfully pale, Snubby. Has something happened?"

"Yes," said Snubby, lying on Miss Pepper's bed again. "That bearded man attacked me, half choked me, and almost flung me down the stairs. I must have hit my head somehow, against the wall, I suppose, when he shook me till my teeth rattled! Loony went for him and bit him – good old Loony!"

Loony growled fiercely, remembering.

"Gosh!" said Barney in horror. "What a brute the man must be! You'd better stay out of his way, Snubby. He's furious with you for getting his letter from the little fisher-boy, Dai, of course. Pity we couldn't read it!"

"I'm staying up here," said Snubby. "I don't know what you can tell Miss Pepper, but today I'm quite definitely keeping out of Sir Richard's way."

"I'll tell her you hit your head and hurt yourself," said Barney, troubled. "I'll suggest to her that you stay up here as it's much quieter than downstairs. Perhaps after tonight those men will go. Do you want any lunch? I could bring a tray up for you."

"No thanks," said Snubby. "I couldn't eat a thing. My tummy feels all of a wobble."

"Bad luck, old son," said Barney, thinking that Snubby must indeed feel terrible not to want his lunch. "Try to get a bit of sleep."

"My head's begun to ache," complained Snubby. "Oooh, Loony, I am glad you went for that spiteful wretch!"

Loony leaped on the bed and Snubby pushed him down. "Sorry – this is Miss Pepper's bed, not mine," he said. "Though I dare say if I went to lie on Diana's bed, she wouldn't mind you coming beside me."

Barney went downstairs and told Miss Pepper that Snubby had somehow hurt his head, and wanted to lie down quietly, and that he didn't want any lunch. Miss Pepper was quite alarmed to hear this and ran up the stairs at once. Barney quickly told the others what had happened and they listened in dismay. Poor old Snubby.

Miss Pepper came down at last and they began their lunch. Miss Pepper was quite worried. "I cannot imagine what Snubby was doing to bang his head like that," she said. "How very sensible of him to want to lie quiet this afternoon – of course my bedroom is just the place! Nobody will disturb him there. I'll pop up after lunch to see if he's all right, and then leave him in peace till teatime. He says he has a most terrible headache, poor boy."

"I bet he'll be all right by teatime," said Roger, eating an enormous chunk of home-cooked meat-pie. "I say, wasn't that little monkey of a Dafydd pleased with his clock!

He must have set that alarm off about twenty times since we gave it to him. I keep hearing it trilling away somewhere or other."

Miss Pepper went up to see Snubby after lunch and was glad to find him fast asleep, with Loony on guard. She tiptoed out of the room, hoping he would sleep till teatime and then feel quite recovered.

"Wouldn't you like to have a swim this afternoon?" Miss Pepper asked the three children. "And lie out in the sun?"

"Sounds great," said Roger. "Let's go a good way along the beach this afternoon, where there are those rock-pools. I bet some of them would be as warm as toast to wallow in."

So they all went over the white sands, and settled down by the rock-pools. The rocks were quite high there, and the tide was going out, leaving warm, shallow pools in which swam grey shrimps.

They swam, and then lay either in the deliciously warm pools, or on the hot sand. Miss Pepper put up a huge sun umbrella, lay down under it and fell asleep.

Barney lay in one of the pools, amused to feel a shoal of little shrimps trying to nibble his leg. He sat up to tell the others and caught sight of two people coming along the sands, deep in talk together.

"Hey!" he said in a low voice. "I spy Sir Richard and the other fellow coming along.

161

Keep your heads down. I wonder where they're going."

The two men walked quickly past on the sand, talking in low voices. "Gone to chat to Morgan and Jim, I suppose," said Barney. "About the doings tonight, whatever they are! What do you bet that one of Morgan's boats is coming in at dead of night with some mysterious 'catch' that they don't want anyone else to see unloaded?"

"Look! Isn't that Dafydd and his goose?" said Roger, in surprise. "Following some way behind the men? I wonder what he's up to? See how close he's keeping to the cliff – as if he doesn't want them to see him?"

"Doing a bit of snooping again, I suppose," said Diana. "You just never know where that child will pop up next!"

They all lay down again in the pool, their heads propped against convenient rocks. Diana yawned. "I think I'd better get out and lie in the sun. I'm almost asleep, and I don't want to wake up choking in the water!"

It was a truly lazy afternoon, and the four, with Miranda too, thoroughly enjoyed it, though they missed Snubby and Loony very much. Miranda sat near Barney on a rock just above his head, sad because she could not sit on his shoulder as usual. But nothing would persuade her to lie in the pool too!

After about an hour Miranda began to chatter quietly, and Barney sat up in the pool. "What's up?" he said. "Is someone coming?"

A small brown face, with a shock of untidy hair above it, peered round the rock at him. It was Dafydd! A long, curving neck was peering round as well, and Barney saw that Waddle was there too.

"Shh!" said Dafydd mysteriously, and then began to point with his finger some way up the beach, jabbing the air with it.

"What is it? What do you want to tell me?" said Barney in a low voice.

"Men," said Dafydd. "Two men. Dafydd see where they go. Dafydd want paper back, and follow men. Up long hole."

"What on earth does he mean?" said Barney to Roger, who was listening. "Do you suppose he went after the men with some wild idea of getting back that letter for us?"

"Up long hole," said Dafydd, nodding. "Dafydd take you."

"This sounds interesting," said Barney. "Let's go with him and see what he means. Wait a bit, though – is that voices? Maybe it's the men coming back. Dafydd, come down here."

Dafydd and the goose scrambled over the rocks to the pool. Dafydd sat beside Barney, his bare feet in the water, the goose paddled solemnly round the pool.

"Men come back," said Dafydd, peering over the rock. Barney pulled him down.

"Keep still," he said, and Dafydd understood and sat quite still, swinging his feet to and fro in the warm pool.

The men passed by once more, on their way back, and were soon out of sight. Dafydd stood up. "Up long hole?" he said, pointing over the sands. Barney and Roger scrambled out of the pool, shook themselves like dogs, and followed the small boy and goose back along the way the men had come.

They came at last to the caves that led into the cliffs, and Dafydd disappeared into one of the two marked DANGEROUS. Barney pulled him back.

"No! This cave is dangerous," he said.

Dafydd obviously didn't understand. He ran right into the cave, and the two boys followed him, feeling rather scared in case part of the roof fell.

"I suppose if the men did go into the cave, it can't be very dangerous!" said Roger.

"Or maybe they labelled it 'Dangerous' themselves," said Barney, grimly. "Perhaps they've got a convenient hiding-place up here!"

"Well it's not much of a cave!" said

Roger, as they came to the end of it.

"Nowhere to hide anything here!"

"Look at Dafydd," said Barney. "He's climbing up that rock – now he's running along a ridge – he's gone!"

So he had! He disappeared halfway along the ridge of rock, and Waddle the goose, left behind on the sandy floor of the cave, sent a sorrowful cackle after him.

Dafydd appeared again, beckoning. They could only just see him, outlined against the dark cave-wall, standing on the ridge.

"Up long hole!" said the small boy. "You come too. Up long hole."

Barney and Roger began to feel excited. They climbed part of the rock at the back of the cave, came to the ridge and walked along it. Halfway along there was a hole in the wall of the rock, and it was through this that Dafydd had disappeared. He now slipped through it again, and the two boys peered after him in the dim light, for the cave was almost dark.

"You come too?" asked Dafydd, and added something in Welsh that they didn't understand.

"Rather!" said Roger, and scrambled through with Miranda at his feet. "Where in the world does this lead to? What a pity we haven't a torch. I say, it really is a long hole, isn't it – as far as we can see, anyway! Come back, Dafydd, we can't go scrambling about in pitch darkness!"

19

Very Exciting!

The two boys and Miranda climbed back into the cave where Waddle greeted them with loud cackles. Dafydd leaped down and joined them.

"Long, long hole," he said. "Men go up long hole. Dafydd too. Long, long, long."

"All very mysterious indeed," said Barney. "Thanks, Dafydd. Did the men see you?"

"Not see Dafydd. Dafydd not get letter," said the small boy, looking doleful. "Dafydd make clock go tr-r-r-r-r-ring, and men came out quick!"

Barney laughed. "You little monkey! You crept behind the men, and set off the alarm! My word, they must have been scared! Good for you, Dafydd. Now you must go home." Dafydd set off across the sands, and the boys went to tell Diana where they had been. She was very interested.

"The men must be smuggling something," she said, "and hiding it up Dafydd's long, long hole. I bet tonight there will be fresh goods to take up there."

"Yes, quite probably," said Barney. "I wonder why they went there today, though. Perhaps to make room for the new stuff? I wish we'd had a torch – we'd have gone right up the very end of the hole. It's a steep passage really, of course, but Dafydd kept calling it a long, long hole! Funny little chap – he went up the rocky cave-wall like a monkey, well like Miranda did, actually, with a spring and a leap and a jump! He must have eyes like a cat; I believe he would even be able to see in the darkness of that passage! It seemed to go up pretty steeply, as far as we could tell."

"Barney – let's watch to see if those men go out tonight," said Roger eagerly. "They'd have to pass fairly near our caravan if they did, and old Loony would be sure to bark. We could creep after them, and see what they take into the cave, if they do go there."

"Yes, I don't see why we shouldn't," said Barney, suddenly excited. "Snubby can come too if he's feeling better – but not you, Di. Miss Pepper would hear you slipping out of your room."

"I do hope old Snubby is better," said Diana. "Fancy that man attacking him like that! The sooner I hear those two men are in prison, the better I'll be pleased. Passing themselves off as a Sir Somebody and a professor!"

Miss Pepper suddenly woke up with a jump and looked at her watch. "Good gracious! It's teatime!" she said. "You run on ahead, children, and tell Mrs Jones to get tea. I'll follow at my own pace."

"Good," said Barney, as they ran off over the sand, "now we can slip upstairs and tell Snubby what we've discovered, without Miss Pepper overhearing."

They found Snubby feeling much better and began to tell him of their afternoon's excitement, but Snubby interrupted.

"Listen!" he said, "something awfully peculiar happened this afternoon, when I was lying here, half asleep. Loony heard a noise first, and barked. I sat up, thinking those men might be coming into the room – but I hardly thought they would, with Loony barking like mad! But the noise didn't come from outside the room – it seemed to come from *inside*."

"What noise?" asked Barney, puzzled.

"I don't exactly know how to describe it," said Snubby. "It was a – a sort of bumping and banging, and it came from that side of the room near the fireplace, but – well, as if it was under the room, sort of muffled."

"Oh Snubby!" said Diana, looking suddenly scared. "It must have been the 'noises' that Mr Jones warned us about, when he said we'd better not have this room, we'd far better have the best room. He said that noises sometimes came in the night but I've not heard any so far. Miss Pepper and I thought it was just nonsense, of course. And now you've heard them!"

"Yes, I certainly heard them," said Snubby. "I didn't dare to get off the bed, and Loony began to bark his head off and ran all round the floor, trying to find out what was making the noises."

"What on earth were they, do you suppose?" said Barney, puzzled. "Is there a door behind the chest – maybe there's a cupboard or something?"

"Look and see," said Snubby, and the three children peered round the back of the great chest. But no door was there, only the stone wall.

"It's a mystery," said Barney. "But we'd better not stay up here discussing it. Miss Pepper will wonder what's up again. Are you coming down to tea, Snubby?"

"Rather. I feel jolly hungry, and I don't particularly want to stay alone in this room of noises any longer," said Snubby. So down they went, to find Miss Pepper patiently awaiting them and a very fine tea on the table.

The four children, with Miranda and Loony, went to have another talk after tea, in the caravan. They shut the door and spoke in low voices. Barney told Snubby of their idea to follow the men, if they went out that night, and see if they went up the "long, long hole".

"I'd like to come but I don't think I will," said Snubby. "I feel a bit shaky now I'm up. I'll tell you what I'll do, though, when you've left the caravan to follow the men, I'll nip upstairs and lie on the couch in the room next to Diana's and wait till I hear them come back – and report to you as soon as you reach the caravan."

"Okay, if you want to," said Barney, understanding quite well that Snubby wasn't particularly anxious to stay all by himself in the caravan that evening!

"Better find our torches," said Roger. "We shall certainly need them. Do you mind if we take Loony with us, Snubby?"

"Er – no," said Snubby, wishing he could say yes, he did mind! He knew he would feel much safer with Loony somewhere near him!

They found their torches and then put on warm jerseys, for the wind had changed and now blew cold. They went to join Miss Pepper, and set off for a short walk in the hills behind the inn. A bird flew up as they walked over the heather, and Barney pointed to it solemnly.

"Is that a crazy corncrake, or a yellow blackbird?" he said. "We'd better ask the Professor when we get back!"

They all began to feel excited when they were back from their walk, and had had supper.

"It's not dark till about ten," said Barney, "so we'll have a game of cards, shall we? Anyway the men are still here, so we needn't worry about them slipping off without us seeing them!"

The two men were walking up and down outside the window well in sight. At about ten they came indoors and went upstairs.

"Getting ready to go, I expect," said Barney. "Come on, we'll be off to the caravan and keep watch. We'll say goodnight to Miss Pepper now."

Miss Pepper and Diana went upstairs to bed. "Good luck!" Diana whispered to the boys as she left. Snubby went off to the caravan with Roger and Barney, who slipped on their warm jerseys again and put their torches into their pockets. Snubby began to wish he was going too, but they wouldn't let him.

"You still look groggy," said Barney. "We don't want you fainting just as we go up the long, long hole, and watch for the men. They won't guess we're watching, so they'll probably come straight out of the front door."

The caravan was in darkness, and the three boys peered out of the window, Miranda too. At about half past ten they heard footsteps, and by the light of the half moon saw the two men coming down the slope.

But wait – there were three men, not two! Barney nudged Roger sharply. "See who the third man is – Mr Jones! I thought he was in this, didn't you?"

"Wait till they've gone round the bend, then we'll follow," said Roger, excited. "Gosh! Fancy Mr Jones going too!"

They slipped out of the caravan with Loony as soon as the men were round the bend, leaving poor Snubby alone. He didn't like being on his own and shot up to the house, creeping up the stairs and going to the room next to Diana's as he planned. He lay down on the couch there, wishing heartily that he had Loony with him.

Meanwhile Roger, Barney, Miranda and Loony were stalking the three men. They were now down on the beach, making their way to Merlin's Cove, where the caves ran back into the cliffs. The moon gave enough light for the men to be clearly seen in front of them, and the boys were careful to keep out of sight by walking close to the cliffs.

"Tide's coming in," said Roger, "and it's going to be pretty high tonight, with that strong wind blowing off the sea. Hello – look! Is that a boat coming ashore?"

They stopped, keeping close to the cliffs, and watched a boat being rowed ashore.

Two men were in it, and the boys felt sure that the man rowing was Morgan. Who was the other?

"Jim, probably, whoever he is," said Barney. "I can't see that they have much in the boat – if they *are* bringing in goods they have smuggled in a fishing catch."

The three men did not go down to the boat when it grounded on the sands but waited while it was pulled up on the beach by Morgan and the second man. Then Morgan and his friend began to lift what seemed to be big packets out of the boat, and went up to the caves with them.

The men took them and disappeared into the cave marked DANGEROUS.

"The one we were in this afternoon, of course!" said Barney.

Then Morgan and his friend went back to the boat and staggered up the beach with more packets, evidently the last ones for they, too, disappeared into the cave. One of them came back and pulled the boat right up to the cave entrance, making it fast.

Then he too went into the cave, and it seemed as if all of them had gone to some hiding-place where the packets were to be placed.

The two boys and Loony went right up to the cave and stood outside, listening. Not a sound was to be heard except the little waves breaking on the sand as the sea came in.

"Come on," said Barney. "Into the cave we go, and up the wall at the back on to that ridge. Maybe we can hear the men if we listen at that hole that goes up and up."

They went in quietly, not switching on their torches at first, for the moon shone into the cave and lit it.

"Up we go!" said Barney, leaping up the wall on to the ridge, and pulling up a most surprised Loony. "And don't let's make any noise, for goodness sake. Loony, not a growl or a bark from you, or you may put us in danger. Here's the hole, Roger. I'll lead the way!"

20

The "Long, Long Hole"

The two boys shone their torches up the hole.

"It goes up and up and up!" said Barney. "It's rather like a shaft, only not so steep, of course. I can't hear a thing; can you?"

"No," said Roger. "The men must be a good way up – come on!"

They began to clamber up the long, steep passage, switching on their torches every now and then to show them their footing. Not a sound could they hear until at last Loony gave a little growl of warning. They snapped off their torches at once.

"Voices!" whispered Barney. "Voices some way in front. We'd better be careful now. Shade your torch with your hand, Roger, when you switch it on. Come on – they're a long way ahead yet. Quiet now, Loony!"

They went on again, listening for any sound from above, but could hear nothing. Either the men had now gone beyond hearing, or were being very quiet. The boys came to a very steep part indeed, and discovered that rough steps had been cut there. They climbed up them, and came to what seemed to be a small cave in the very heart of the cliff. They sat down to rest for a moment, panting from the long, steep climb. Loony ran round, sniffing here and there.

"Loony! Come here! Miranda? Where have you gone?" whispered Barney, switching on his torch and shining it round the little cave. "*Now* where are they, Roger? I can hear them, but can't see them!"

He got up cautiously, and went farther into the cave. He found the two scraping about behind a big rock, unearthing the bones of some small animal. "Leave that alone!" whispered Barney. "Come with us. We're going on up the hole."

Miranda leaped on to his shoulder and Loony reluctantly left his find. Once more they all scrambled up the steep passage, which was, in truth, more like a "long, long hole", as Dafydd had said.

"Have you any idea of the direction we're going in?" asked Roger.

"No – except that we seem to slant to the left all the time," said Barney. "We must have got beyond the cliffs by now and be burrowing up the hills at the back of them."

They heard noises again a little later and stopped to listen. The noises went on and on, and sounded as if things were being moved or stacked. They could also hear voices.

"I bet they're opening those packets and stacking the contents somewhere," said Roger. "Shall we go any nearer?"

"Yes – but I think perhaps only one of us," said Barney. "You stay here with Loony and Miranda, and I'll go as near as I dare. Keep your hand on Loony's collar."

Barney went on up the steep passage, and soon the sound of voices was quite loud. Counting was going on – "100 – 200 – 300" – Barney heard. He looked up the passage, which was not so steep here, and saw a bright circle of light not far ahead.

"That's where the passage stops and the hiding-place is," thought Barney. "They're all up there together. I can hear Morgan's deep voice now – I wish I could hear what he's saying but I hardly dare creep any closer."

He stayed for about ten minutes, listening to the sound of things being shifted about and stacked, and voices arguing. Then suddenly he got a shock.

The men were coming back, and the lamp or whatever it was that he could see shining some way up the passage, in the hiding-place, was suddenly switched off. The beams from torches appeared instead! Barney scrambled back to Roger quickly, finding it much easier to go down than it had been to climb up!

"Roger – they're coming down!" he whispered. "Pretty quickly, too. Come on. Where's Miranda?"

"She slipped off," said Roger. "I didn't see her go. She's probably gone down again."

They went down farther, hoping to see Miranda waiting for them, but she was nowhere to be seen. Loony didn't like slithering down any better than he liked scrambling up! They came to the little round cave where Loony and Miranda had unearthed the bones. "There she is!" said Barney, exasperated, shining his torch on the little monkey.

She leaped up to a jutting piece of rock and chattered at him. "Come here at once," ordered Barney in a low voice, but Miranda chose to be annoying, and sat up on the rock, swaying about and chattering all kinds of nonsense.

"We'll have to go on, Barney," said Roger. "I can hear the men getting quite near."

"Well, I'm not leaving Miranda," said Barney. "Come on – let's hide behind that rock where Loony unearthed those bones. The men will never guess anyone is here; they don't know they were followed."

"All right," said Roger, feeling uneasy as the men's voices grew louder and louder. He and Loony went quickly to the big rock and stood silently behind it, Loony pressing against his legs. Miranda at once dropped on to Barney's shoulder and put her tiny paws down his neck.

The voices came very near, and the sound of the men's feet was almost deafening as they slipped and slithered down the steep, rocky passage. Loony couldn't help giving little growls as they passed the entrance of the small cave in which the boys were hiding.

Roger tapped him sharply, afraid that the men would hear, and stop to investigate. But mercifully they didn't, and soon the sound of their voices and feet grew less and less, until finally the boys could hear no sound at all.

"It's all right now – we can go," said Barney, relieved, and switched on his torch. "Miranda, take your hands out of my neck, you tickle terribly. And stay on my shoulder, or I'll never bring you out on an adventure again!"

The boys went down the hole, slithering over very steep parts, making far more noise than when they went up! They came at last to the end of the hole, and stood on the ridge of rock on the wall of the big cave. The moon shone into the cave – and what a shock the boys had!

The moon now shone, not on white sand, but on heaving water! Water that was already as high as the ridge they stood on! It caught the moonlight at the entrance and then shimmered in the light of the boys' torches, at the dark rear end of the cave.

"The tide's come in to the cave – right in – and it's still rising!" said Barney, in horror. "I never thought of that. It's swept into this cave – and all the other caves, of course – and the wind is piling up the waves high enough to swamp the lot. What shall we do?"

"I reckon the men only just got away in time," said Roger. "But, of course, they had a boat. Look out – that wave will sweep us off the ridge!"

They leaped back a little way up the hole just in time to avoid being swept away as an enormous wave splashed right over the ridge. They retreated back up the hole, scared.

"Well," said Barney, "it certainly looks as if we're going to be penned up here for some time, because the tide isn't full for an hour or two. It's that strong wind that's making it so high. Snubby will be waiting and waiting for us to get back and he'll be worried stiff."

"I say – let's go back up the hole and see what the men have hidden in that hidy-hole, or whatever it is, right at the top of the passage," said Roger, excited. "Come on – it's a fine chance for us, Barney! We know the men can't come back, because they wouldn't be able to get through the water in the cave."

"You know – that's an idea!" said Barney, delighted. "A really good idea! If we find out what's hidden there, we can go to the police tomorrow and tell them, not only about the men, but about what they've hidden, and where it is! If only we didn't have to make that awful climb all over again!"

"Oh, come on! It won't seem so bad this time because we don't need to be afraid of the men hearing us," said Roger, and Loony barked at the excitement in his voice.

So back they went, up the long, shaft-like passage – and certainly this time it did not seem so long, for they could go as carelessly as they liked and not be afraid of making even the slightest noise! They let Loony bark, and allowed Miranda to scamper ahead as much as she liked.

They came to the last part of the passage, which was steeper than ever.

"There's a rope-ladder here, at the very end," panted Barney, shining his torch in front of him.

Roger saw a strong rope-ladder stretching up from the end of the rocky passage to the entrance of the hiding-place. He held Loony while Barney went up the rope with Miranda. Then he went up too, leaving Loony below.

The boys stared round at the hiding-place. It was about three metres square, a natural hole in the rock that someone had made into a kind of cell by chipping the walls smooth, and the floor level. It was stacked with oblong packets, marked with numbers. Except for a few empty bottles which held drink of some kind, and a couple of old rugs, there was nothing else to be seen.

"Gosh – what a wonderful hidy-hole!" said Roger, looking round. "I wonder who first discovered it. Barney, what do you suppose is in those packets?"

"I think I know all right!" said Barney. "They're packets of bank-notes. Stolen bank-notes that can't be passed for some considerable time because the numbers are known – but which could be shipped across to Ireland easily enough, perhaps from this Welsh coast – or stored till the hoo-ha and excitement has died down, and then used some time in the future!"

"I say! But there must be millions here!" said Roger, amazed. He patted a big packet. "This will be about the only time in my life that I shall ever be able to say I have laid my hands on hundreds of thousands of pounds! Barney – now I see why those men got Mr Jones into their power. They badly wanted good headquarters down here on this coast, where they could bring their stuff by boat and hide it, and then take them away again by boat – over to Ireland, perhaps, as you say!"

"Yes. Or help themselves to a packet or two when they knew they could get rid of the notes undetected in London, or some other big town!" said Barney. "Do you remember the last bank raid, Roger, where the thieves ambushed the driver of a bank van and drove off in the van with hundreds of thousands of pounds? Not one note has been traced so far – and I wouldn't mind betting it's all here!"

Roger's heart began to beat fast as he glanced round at the stacked packets again.

"Could we open one just to see?" he said.

"Better not," said Barney. "We'll tell Miss Pepper tomorrow – and I'll telephone my father. He'll get on to the London police. I shouldn't think the village policeman here could deal with it."

Roger sat down on a pile of the packets. "To think I may be sitting on half a million pounds!" he said. "Oh Barney – I wish we could get out of here and tell everyone! To think we're penned up here for hours because of that high tide."

Barney glanced all round the little room, and then happened to look upwards. What he saw so astounded him that he stood as if turned into a statue, staring, staring. Roger was quite alarmed.

"What's the matter?" he said, and looked upwards too. He was as amazed as Barney at what he saw.

"A trapdoor! A wooden trapdoor! Set in the roof of this funny round hole. Barney! Let's open it and get out and see where we are. Quick, Barney!"

Barney was as excited as he was, but more cautious. "Wait a bit, wait a bit! We don't know where the trapdoor leads to, ass.

We might walk straight into trouble! Shut up, Loony, shut up barking! Gosh, we've excited him now, too, and he'll bark the place down. I'd better go down the ladder and drag him up here. Perhaps he'll be quiet then."

They stacked up the packets high enough to reach the trapdoor, and then climbed up them. Both boys raised their arms and pushed at the wooden trapdoor, which fitted closely into a square of the roof. But it would not budge.

"Must be fastened on the other side!" panted Barney. "Try again, Roger!"

They tried again, banging at the trapdoor in their impatience, making a tremendous noise.

"I expect it opens into some deserted cellar or pit," said Roger. "Probably nobody will hear us, Barney. Try again! Oh, Loony, do be quiet!"

"I suppose the men prefer to use the cave way when they bring the money in," said Barney, taking a rest, "because it's so easy to bring it by boat. Nobody would suspect a boat going out by night, and Merlin's Cove would be quite deserted then. But the men don't need to help themselves to the money by way of the cave and the hole. When they want it, they've only got to open the trapdoor and drop neatly down, collect what they want, and go back through the trapdoor again. Very clever!"

"Let's try the trapdoor again," said Roger. "We might use one of these packages as a battering-ram – they're solid enough! Do stop barking, Loony, it's quite deafening in here!"

The two boys stood on the packages – and then they suddenly leaped down in fright. Loony growled fiercely, making Miranda jump in fear on to Barney's shoulder.

"Someone's opening the trapdoor!" said Roger. "I can hear noises up above. Oh, gosh, Barney, it's not those men is it? We're trapped if it is. We've no getaway at all!"

21

The Trapdoor Opens!

And now, how was Snubby getting on, lying alone in the little room next to Miss Pepper's, missing Loony very much – listening anxiously for the two men to return to their room nearby?

He was quite determined to creep behind the big couch he was on, if he heard so much as a footstep! But he heard nothing at all for what seemed like hours, and at last fell asleep very suddenly indeed.

Diana too, in the next room, was fast asleep, but Miss Pepper was still reading a book. At last she yawned, shut her book and turned off her bedside light. She was just going to sleep when she thought she heard a little noise. She opened her eyes and listened – no – it must have been an owl outside.

She fell asleep, and then awoke again some time later. She sat up. What had woken her? She listened intently. There – a noise – it came again and again. It almost sounded as if it were in the room!

Miss Pepper was not easily scared, but her hand was trembling a little as she switched on her light again. Diana woke up, as the light illuminated the room.

"Are you all right, Miss Pepper?" she asked sleepily, thinking it was the middle of the night, although she hadn't really been asleep very long. "Ooh – what's that?"

"I don't know," said Miss Pepper, puzzled. "I heard noises but there doesn't seem to be anything to cause them."

"Oh, Miss Pepper, they must be the noises Mr Jones told us about!" said Diana. "He didn't want us to have this room because of them – nor did Mrs Jones."

"Oh yes," said Miss Pepper. "But I really thought that was only a bit of nonsense. There, did you hear that? A deep-down sort of noise – bump!"

"Yes," said Diana, scared. "And I don't like it very much. Where's it coming from, Miss Pepper?"

"I don't know," said Miss Pepper, getting out of bed, and looking into every corner. Diana thought she was very, very brave! *Bump! Boomp! Bump!*

"It's coming from the old chest!" said Diana, with a little scream.

"No, dear, no," said Miss Pepper. "Don't be silly. There's nothing in the chest but our clothes. You know that."

Miss Pepper went to the door of their room and opened it, looking up and down the passageway to make sure that the three boys were not playing some sort of silly joke in the middle of the night to scare her and Diana. They could be very annoying at times!

But no – no one was there. She noticed that the door of the next room was a little open and went to it. Was anyone hiding there?

She had the surprise of her life when she saw Snubby fast asleep there, sprawled on the big sofa, still in his day clothes! What on earth was he doing there? She went over and shook him. He awoke in a hurry, scared stiff, thinking the men had got hold of him!

"Why are you here, Snubby? Did you hear any noises?" asked Miss Pepper, wondering if by any chance she could be dreaming it all.

"Ooh – you did frighten me," said Snubby. "What noises? No, I've heard none but I did hear some when I was resting in your room today, sort of bump-boomp-bump!"

"Yes – that's what we've been hearing, Diana and I," said Miss Pepper. "Come and listen, Snubby."

So Snubby joined Diana in the next room and they all listened. But they could hear absolutely nothing at all now.

"Funny!" said Snubby. "Not a sound to be heard. Can I sleep on your couch at the foot of the bed, Miss Pepper? To – to see that you're safe, you know."

Miss Pepper smiled a little. "Of course, Snubby, but now tell me why you were sleeping in the next room, instead of in the caravan with the others? What's happened? Have you quarrelled?"

"I can't tell you just yet, Miss Pepper," said Snubby awkwardly. "Tell you tomorrow, perhaps."

He snuggled down on the sofa, with a blanket thrown over him, and Diana and Miss Pepper got into bed again. The light was switched off, and they all lay in darkness, hoping to goodness that there would be no more disturbing noises. None came, and one by one the three fell asleep once more.

Some time later Snubby woke again and sat up, astonished. He heard a most surprising noise – so surprising that he thought he must have been dreaming. But no, there it was again – *wuff-wuff-wuff!* It was Loony barking!

"Miss Pepper! I can hear Loony barking!" he cried, shaking her awake. "But it can't be! Di, wake up! Can you hear Loony?"

Now they were all awake and listening. *Wuff-wuff-wuff!* Yes, that was Loony all right. But where was he? The barking sounded near and yet muffled.

"This is really mysterious," said Miss Pepper, worried. "Where in the world can Loony be?"

Then loud noises came – *Bang! Bang-bang-bang!* They sounded almost as if someone was knocking at a door somewhere, very fiercely indeed.

"The noises are coming from the chest," said Diana, almost in tears.

"Let's move it out," said Snubby. "I thought the same myself this afternoon, when I heard them. Come on – help me, both of you – it's dreadfully heavy!"

It certainly was but they managed to shift it at last, and there, where it had stood, was a wooden trapdoor, shut tightly down!

"Gosh – look at that! No wonder they didn't want you to have this room!" said Snubby. "This trapdoor must be used for something secret, for whatever dirty work those two men are doing! There – I can hear Loony again! And that's Barney's voice – listen!"

"But – but who put them down there and shut the trapdoor on them?" said Miss Pepper, overcome with amazement. "I never heard of such a thing in my life! Can we lift up the trapdoor, Snubby? Oh, dear – I feel as if this must be a dream!"

"Can't be," said Snubby. "It's much too noisy. Gosh, they're banging at the trapdoor again. They couldn't open it while the chest was standing on it, of course. Hey, wait a bit, I'll pull this handle – ah – up she comes!"

And the trapdoor gradually lifted as Snubby and Diana pulled at the iron handle!

Down below there was great consternation, of course. Barney and Roger were absolutely horrified to see the trapdoor being raised from the other side! They at once thought that somehow the two men were there, and that now they would be discovered – and properly trapped. They ran to the rope-ladder and began to climb down it. But Loony wouldn't come. He began to bark excitedly as the trapdoor opened, and he heard Snubby's beloved voice.

"Hey!" called Snubby, looking down the hole. "Loony! What on earth are you doing there! Loony!"

Loony nearly went mad, trying to jump as high as the trapdoor and failing miserably. Barney and Roger and Miranda paused when they heard Loony's happy barking, and Snubby's voice.

"That can't be Snubby opening the trapdoor!" said Barney, amazed. "But it's his voice! Quick, let's get back into the little room and see." So back up the rope-ladder they went and saw Snubby peering through the open trapdoor, and Loony almost mad with joy.

"Snubby! How did you get there?" yelled Roger. "Where are you?"

"In Miss Pepper's room. Under the old chest," said Snubby, getting muddled in his excitement. "But I say – how did you get down there? Gosh, this really must be a dream. Hand Loony up, will you, before he goes stark raving mad!"

Loony was handed up, and promptly did go completely mad, tearing round and round the room, leaping on the beds and barking at the top of his voice. Miranda leaped through the trapdoor too, and poor Miss Pepper's bedroom became a complete madhouse as the two animals chased round and round.

Barney and Roger climbed through the trapdoor, helped by Snubby, and were soon sitting on the beds, laughing and most relieved at their extraordinary escape.

"Well! To think that passage from the cave led right up to Miss Pepper's bedroom!" said Barney. "I never even dreamed it would go to the inn – but of course now I think of it, it went so steeply up a slope and veered this way all the time right to the hill that rises up against the back walls. So easy to make a secret entrance! Everything fits in beautifully now, the men staying here, and wanting this bedroom because it's the entrance to their hidy-hole – and . . ."

"I simply cannot imagine what you are

talking about," said poor Miss Pepper. "Will you kindly enlighten me?"

"Oh don't go all starchy, Miss Pepper darling," said Snubby hugging her. "We've kept a secret from you – listen."

And he and the others poured out their strange story to the amazed Miss Pepper. She could hardly believe it.

"Why didn't you tell me anything of this?" she demanded. "I would have taken you all away from here at once."

"That's just why we didn't tell you!" said Roger. "We couldn't bear to leave in the middle of something mysterious like this. Isn't it exciting, Miss Pepper?"

"It's certainly exciting," said poor Miss Pepper, quite overcome. "I wonder why it is that I can never go away with you children without getting mixed up in something really undesirable!"

"But Miss Pepper, don't you think it's desirable to catch thieves?" said Barney. "Those two men must be two of the cleverest in the country – and we've found out! Oughtn't we do something about it at once?"

"Oh dear – in the middle of the night?" said Miss Pepper. "Well, perhaps we ought."

"Roger, you and Snubby see if you can get some of those packages up into the bedroom," said Barney. "And I'll go down quietly to the telephone, and wake up my poor father and tell him to inform Scotland Yard, or his local police if he thinks it's best, of our discoveries."

So, while Snubby fetched a rope from the caravan to fix to the strong handle of the trapdoor, and then slid down it to pass up packages to Roger, Barney went quietly down to the telephone, woke up his astounded father and told him the news. He kept an ear open for the two men coming back, but not until he had put down the receiver and gone upstairs again did he hear quiet footsteps.

He slipped into Miss Pepper's room, shushing the others, and listened until he heard the men's door closing quietly shut. Then he slipped out again, and came back looking so triumphant that Miss Pepper was astonished.

"What have you been up to now, Barney?" she said.

"Nothing much," said Barney. "The men left the key of their room outside in the lock, so I just slipped out and locked them in. They will have to wait there until the police come and let them out because I've got the key in my pocket!"

It was very late when at last the three boys, with Loony and Miranda, went down to the caravan to get a little sleep. Diana and Miss Pepper crawled into bed, but could not go to sleep for a long time because they had to talk and talk and talk!

"It will be an exciting day tomorrow!" said Diana – and it certainly was! Two cars arrived about nine o'clock, full of plain-clothes police, and poor Mr Jones had the shock of his life when they appeared in his kitchen!

The two men also had a terrible shock when they found their door well and truly locked from the outside – and were faced by four sturdy policemen when at last it was opened!

"What's the meaning of this!" blustered Sir Richard angrily – but he calmed down at once when an inspector reached out and tugged off his beard!

"Ah, George Higgins," said the Inspector. "I thought so. You look more like yourself now, George. You and your friend took some fine-sounding names, didn't you! Would you please come with us – and your friend too. Don't worry about the bank notes; we'll take care of those!"

And within twenty minutes the police cars had gone, taking with them the false Sir Richard and the equally bogus Professor Hallinan, both of whom they had been looking for for some considerable time. Alas, Mr Jones went with them!

Poor Mr Jones! As Mrs Jones said, "He's not bad is my Llewellyn, they lent him money to buy the inn. How was he to know they were bad men – a Sir and a professor? And his cooking, it was so good, so very good cooking!"

Morgan and Jim were also paid visits by the police, and disappeared from the little village of Penrhyndendraith for a long time.

Mrs Jones, in tears, begged Miss Pepper not to leave. "I have no money!" she wept. "Stay here with the children and let me have your payment. What else shall I do? My cooking is fair, not very good cooking like Mr Jones's, but it is not bad. Have pity on me, Miss Pepper."

"Well, we don't really want to leave," said Miss Pepper. "We can none of us go home at the moment – and I'm very, very sorry about all this, Mrs Jones. We'll stay for another two weeks at least. And let's hope it will be a holiday, not a peculiar mystery to be solved, with noises in the night and all the rest of it!"

And a holiday it was, with sunny days, blue seas, white sands – boating, fishing, swimming, walking! All the four went as brown as berries, and they were joined by another boy, small and just as brown. Dafydd tagged on to them, with his faithful goose Waddle – and his precious alarm clock!

Enid Blyton

THE BARNEY MYSTERIES

Join Barney, Roger, Diana and Snubby
on their mystery-solving adventures!

ISBN 978-1-84135-728-7

ISBN 978-1-84135-729-4

ISBN 978-1-84135-730-0

ISBN 978-1-84135-731-7

ISBN 978-1-84135-732-4

ISBN 978-1-84135-733-1

Enid Blyton

THE ADVENTUROUS FOUR

Follow the adventures of Tom, twins Pippa
and Zoe, and their friend Andy who has a sailing
boat on which the four love to go exploring.

ISBN 978-1-84135-734-8

ISBN 978-1-84135-735-5

ISBN 978-1-84135-736-2

Enid Blyton

THE YOUNG ADVENTURERS

Read all about the exciting adventures of
Nick, Katie, Laura and their friends.

ISBN 978-1-84135-737-9

ISBN 978-1-84135-738-6

ISBN 978-1-84135-739-3

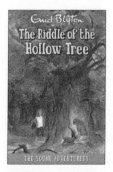

ISBN 978-1-84135-740-9

ISBN 978-1-84135-741-6

ISBN 978-1-84135-742-3

Enid Blyton

The Secret Series

Follow the adventures of Mike, Peggy and
Nora as they discover a secret island, explore
the heart of Africa and unravel the mysteries of
the Killimooin Mountains...

PB ISBN 978-1-84135-673-0
HB ISBN 978-1-84135-748-5

PB ISBN 978-1-84135-675-4
HB ISBN 978-1-84135-749-2

PB ISBN 978-1-84135-676-1
HB ISBN 978-1-84135-750-8

PB ISBN 978-1-84135-677-8
HB ISBN 978-1-84135-751-5

PB ISBN 978-1-84135-674-7
HB ISBN 978-1-84135-752-2

PB ISBN 978-1-84135-678-5
HB ISBN 978-1-84135-753-9

Enid Blyton

Family Adventures

ISBN 978-1-84135-645-7

ISBN 978-1-84135-646-4

ISBN 978-1-84135-647-1

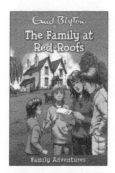

ISBN 978-1-84135-648-8

ISBN 978-1-84135-649-5

ISBN 978-1-84135-650-1

Enid Blyton
ADVENTURE
OMNIBUSES

ISBN 978-1-84135-588-7

As soon as Peter, Pam and their cousin Brock
hear about the strange castle by the sea they are
determined to solve its mystery, but an unknown
enemy awaits them in the castle's secret and
ghostly passages...

ISBN 978-1-84135-587-0

Bob and Mary decide to search their Granny's
house for a necklace they see in a family portrait.
But will their big cousin Ralph help or hinder them?

Enid Blyton

ADVENTURE
OMNIBUSES

ISBN 978-1-84135-589-4

Discover the trials and tribulations of six
cousins who are forced to share life on a country
farm, how they learn to adapt their lives to suit
one another, and the scrapes and adventures
they have together.

Enid Blyton

Enid Blyton was born in London in 1897. Her childhood was spent in Beckenham, Kent and as a child she began to write poems, stories and plays.

She trained as a teacher, but devoted most of her life to writing for children. Her first book was a collection of poems, published in 1922. In 1926 she began to write a weekly magazine for children called *Sunny Stories*, and it was here that many of her most popular stories and characters first appeared.

She wrote more than 700 books for children, many of which have been translated into over 30 languages.